LITTLE LIFE STORIES

LITTLE LIFE STORIES

BY

SIR HARRY JOHNSTON

Short Story Index Reprint Series

 BOOKS FOR LIBRARIES PRESS
FREEPORT, NEW YORK

First Published 1923
Reprinted 1970

STANDARD BOOK NUMBER:
8369-3558-6

LIBRARY OF CONGRESS CATALOG CARD NUMBER:
79-122725

PRINTED IN THE UNITED STATES OF AMERICA

CONTENTS

	PAGE
THE PITUITARY GLAND	1
THE CHALK-PIT	11
THE YOUNG MESSIAH	19
MRS. DOUBLEDAY	30
EDITH STALLIBRASS; OR, THE SIN OF UNSELFISHNESS	41
JAMES MACGEOCHAN ("JIM MAGEEN")	49
"THE REV. D. MACAULAY"	61
THE END OF THE DAY	77
THE JEWELS AT DAVENSHAM CASTLE	90
NOT WHAT YOU MIGHT HAVE EXPECTED	105
"GOOD-NIGHT, OLD MAN!"	118
FREDERICK'S REMORSE	131
SIR MATTHEW CASELY BROMPTON	148
"OLD ARTHUR"	153
SAMUEL GWILLYM	161
JEANNETTE SIDEBOTHAM	169
MRS. MUGGRIDGE	178
LADY ISOBEL DRUMHAVEN	184
THE BROWSMITHS	189
ADELA TOTWORTHY	200
THE TASK	209

LITTLE LIFE STORIES

THE PITUITARY GLAND

ELEUSINE BRAND, between the ages of eight and ten, lost both her parents. They were Quakers —Quaker bakers—inheriting great wealth, second cousins, and descendants on both sides of a Norfolk family of Quakers, who built up in the eighteenth and first half of the nineteenth centuries an immense business in bread. In one form and another—limited companies chiefly— they are at the back of the bread business of to-day, in spite of war fluctuations.

Somehow in the course of two hundred years this Brand stock had, by inbreeding or some such process of specialisation and refinement, become delicate in constitution. The two young cousins, each an only child, and both colossally rich, fell etherally in love with one another in their teens. The girl—Susannah—was born in 1877, and allowed to marry her second cousin Jonathan (who was only twenty-five) in 1898.

She died in 1906, when giving birth to her third child; and her still-young husband (Jonathan Brand) was a victim to an influenza outbreak in 1910. Their two younger children also died in childhood, so Eleusiné, by the time she was ten, had become sole heiress to their united fortunes—sunk in cornfields, farms, bakeries, biscuit manufactories, Norwegian soda mines, and light railways—of something near £1,200,000.

By the wills of her parents she was not permitted, save in the event of the firm's dissolution, to draw this capital out of it; but she could do as she liked with the interest on its investment. This at an average of 8 per cent. was £48,000 a year; and at the age of twenty-one she was mistress of this income.

During her minority, though she had as expensive an education as could be given to a girl, the guardianship of her father's sister (also well to do), two governesses, a Swedish instructress in hygiene, a household, three gardeners, and numerous pet dogs and horses, her annual expenditure in Norfolk scarcely exceeded £10,000 a year; so that, after accounting for subscriptions to a thousand outside charities which prey on the crumbs from the rich, about £30,000 was annually saved during her minority. At twenty-one, therefore, she had a fund of about £300,000 to do as she liked with, even after wartime taxation had been discounted.

She grew to be tallish, but not lanky, had a beautiful complexion, fine eyes, and well-marked eyebrows. These last were often puckered on the brow as if she were constantly reflecting on the enigmas of life.

During her girlhood she lived rather secluded in the Norfolk home. Her Quakeress aunt was timidly adverse to society. But, after her eighteenth birthday, Eleusiné began to assert herself more, and evinced a remarkable bent towards the study of surgery (beginning with her dogs), medicine, comparative anatomy, and the chemistry of bread-making. She heard one day, when they had come up for a glimpse of the London season, mention made of the College of Surgeons. Soon afterwards she went to her Aunt Euphemia—Aunt Effie—and asked to be taken there. . . .

"But, my dear Lucy" (that was the family shortening of Eleusiné)—"my dear Lucy, I—I—hardly think—it —— However, I'll consult your other guardian."

The other guardian, a male, deeply versed in biscuit-making—also a Quaker—said, "*Best* education a girl could possibly have!"

So, arrangements being made, Eleusiné went there two days a week and gave herself up at first to the study of war wounds. Nothing of this kind connected with the poor, tortured human body seemed to repel her. The surgeons and students working there with war-time intermittence were at first only conscious of her beautiful face (vacuous girlhood being nearly shed), her slim body suitably clad for such studies, and the fact that she was doggedly followed by a middle-aged aunt and some sort of governess. Eleusiné shrank from no exposure of anatomy; the governess was hardened in sensibility (though innately bored); but poor Aunt Effie felt everything terribly, and for some time could hardly restrain a sense of nausea at the sight of blood, even when congealed, of fat, of sodden flesh, and the coarse smell of preserving alcohol.

When Eleusiné had passed her nineteenth year, Miss Euphemia Brand could no longer endure the involuntary apprenticeship to surgical studies. Reluctantly, and feeling still, though vainly, that some stand should be made by the family or the firm, she allowed Eleusiné to give up the study of music and go three times a week when in London to the great Museum in Lincoln's Inn Fields;

or alternatively to certain hospitals recommended by the amused and interested surgeons, who saw in her niece a possible parallel to Florence Nightingale.

There was woe in Mayfair when people's minds were lifted off the problem of how to win the War, and returned young men were looking out for well-dowered wives—woe at the difficulty in catching Miss Brand, this great heiress—"A *million* of money, my dear!"—who had just come out. She had been presented at the first Court held after the War. But she disliked dancing, did not—the daring said—know *how* to dance. She was certainly good looking, but *far* too serious; exacting in conversation; sarcastic over tennis tournaments; and only expanded and became really lovely when in conversation with elderly philosophers and physiologists. When the younger followers of science realized that, first and foremost, they were *men,* and passed from politeness to courtship, she soon withdrew herself from their society.

One man in quite other circles was drawn within her radius—the young Marquis of Medmenham. He had inherited the title in the early part of the War. His father and grandfather had shockingly mismanaged the property of the marquisate, and he had five sisters and a mother living. When these were provided for, there remained to him little more than ten thousand a year. The chief house of his family had been let to an enormously wealthy coal merchant.

Lord Medmenham was big, strong, and healthy—a rather material-minded young man at the end of the War, when he was about twenty-seven. His education had really only just begun with his entrance into the Army

THE PITUITARY GLAND

at the age of twenty; he had learnt nothing of any practical use at the first of our public schools. But he had fought through nearly all the War as a cavalry officer turned foot slogger, had become an amateur engineer whom few motors could baffle, a road-maker, a bricklayer, and a gunsmith. He had led two or three forlorn hopes in an uncommonly cheery manner, but had been wounded at the beginning of the great German push in March, 1918. However, he recovered in time to join in the splendid, exhilarating winter march through Belgium to Cologne at the beginning of the Armistice.

Eleusiné Brand and her fortune seemed just the thing for him. . . . Any amount of money, and, hang it all! "Money coming from bread and biscuits, corn and fields to grow it in; you couldn't have a much more decent origin for wealth!" He himself had never appreciated biscuits as he had done in the trenches—"mixed" and "Albert."

He got presented to Eleusiné at one of the rare dances entailed by her coming out. He himself danced well, but Eleusiné had pretexted a strained ankle, and sat out— on a nicely shaded balcony where talking was easier in the seclusion and scented gloom of azaleas and lilac. Yet as the weeks went by he felt he was making little progress. Eleusiné did not snub him or fall into a conclusive silence as she did with some men. He even thought in the half-light of the bower she looked steadily into his face and sized him up; nor did she blush and turn her head aside when their looks met. Accompanied by her aunt, she came down to Ranelagh to see him play polo, and showed perhaps more interest in his polo pony than in him. . . .

"What do you *really* care about?" he asked one day in despair. It was a day in June, 1920.

"*I?* Well, at present it is the Pituitary Gland that absorbs me most. I feel if we could only understand *that,* and all it means, we——" And her voice faded away before the inquiry of a servant.

The Pituitary Gland?

He called on a surgeon in Harley Street. . . .

"I'm afraid there's something wrong with my Pituitary Gland," he began.

"Well, then, my dear young sir"—the doctor glanced down at the card—"my dear Lord, we can do nothing for you in Harley Street, for we haven't unravelled its mysteries. Do you know where it is?"

"Somewhere in my head, I've heard. Wounded in the neck and back of head, 1918. All right now—and yet, I don't know——"

"Go along to the Museum of the College of Surgeons. . . . Here, I'll give you my card." He scribbled something. "Take that to the hall porter and look up the gland. I don't think *you've* any cause for anxiety, judging from your *eyes, complexion, voice-timbre,* and *hand-grip.*"

At the College of Surgeons, Lord Medmenham had two agreeable surprises. The hall porter had been a company sergeant at Péronne. . . . "Remembered him well." . . . And the curator. . . . Well, this *was* a surprise. The curator was a great surgeon who had come to look at his wound—at Abbeville——

"My dear chap! *Who'd* ever have thought it! Right

THE PITUITARY GLAND

as a trivet. Oh, I've forgotten all about my wound—dare say I'll have a twinge or two, when the weather gets beastly again. Wasn't about *that* I came along here. I've been told you can tell me all there is to know about —about—here, I've got it written down—'the Pituitary Gland'—in the skull, don't you know. . . ."

"Yes. I know the Pituitary Gland. It's my specialty. It's strange how interest in it is spreading. Ever since I gave those lectures, there's been a down on the poor thing. . . ."

"Don't say so? You mean I'm not the first? . . ."

"*First?* About the fifty-first. . . . There's Professor Jenkins and young Snodgrass—and a very charming young woman. . . ."

"You mean Miss Brand?"

"I do. Do you know her?"

"Yes; we've met. But let me see the bally thing, *if* you've got the time to spare. . . ."

They went. The preparations were in glass bottles on shelves in a small room opening out of the gallery on the first floor. For a wonder, there was no one there. . . .

"I'm wasting your time awfully, I know . . ." said Lord Medmenham on his second visit, on which, after meticulously staring at the small bottles, he had evinced a desire to study the larger mammals.

"You are. But there's no need to. You know your way about by now, and, if you don't there are catalogues on every floor, and all our attendants are civil spoken. You have but to ask your way. . . ."

"I call it *awfully* good of you. I am *dead nuts* on this Pituitary Gland, and when I've exhausted *that,* I should like to go much further. . . . Put on somebody's white overall—or bring one of my own—like a cricket umpire's—and go up to the fifth—or is it the sixth?—floor, and see a hippopotamus's bowels or whatever it is you're gloating over. But if I'm going to waste your time, that stops me *dead.* . . ."

"Well, don't let it. Come here and study as much as you like. We'll take no notice of you. . . ."

On the third occasion of his visits, Lord Medmenham was in luck. He had donned a white overall, put his hat and stick in the vestibule, and as he passed the exhibits of the Pituitary Gland he thrilled with delight at seeing Eleusiné—alone—at work. The companion was studying the Odontological collection in the basement. Her employer was making several very careful drawings, and was quite indifferent to the person in white passing by.

An hour afterwards Lord Medmenham, without his overall, passed her again, and said, as if she were in the way, *"Excuse* me. . . ."

She looked up, and vague recognition came into her eyes. . . . "Why? . . . I—did not know—you. . . ."

"Oh, *how* d'you do! Jolly place this, isn't it? Devil of a lot to see. I'm doin' intestines just now. . . ."

"I didn't know you *cared.* . . . Oh, here is my friend, Miss Braithwaite! She's been studying teeth. . . . Let me introduce you. . . . Lord Medmenham. . . . I suppose, Braithy, it's lunch-time?"

"*Jove*," said Medmenham, "*so* it is! *Do* let me take you both to lunch. I'll ask the chap at the door to call a taxi. . . . Are you coming back here afterwards?"

"Of course; and, what is more, I must be back in an hour. . . ."

The eventual outcome was that she accepted him. Not the first time he asked; not the second. But they got used that summer and autumn to meeting and seeing one another; and when they didn't meet, through the autumn shoots, Eleusiné in Norfolk felt she wanted him. She was increasingly lonely in her great wealth and inapproachability, and the very defences which had been raised as to her disposal of her money (how it could not be withdrawn from the firms of Bakerhood and Biscuitry in which it was invested), and how she intended to apply two-thirds of her income to the unremunerative purposes of science or benevolence, proved effectual; and her lack of interest in frivolous pastimes did the rest in keeping visitors away.

Lord Medmenham, who in the beginning of his courtship thought of her great fortune as the main asset to be pursued, came, month succeeding month, to want to marry her for herself. . . .

One slumberous autumn day in mid-October she was sauntering down the drive to the gates. She saw him come through them in a motor—hardly knew all that happened next. . . . He was walking by her side through the fern, out of sight of man—saying something impetuously. . . . There was only one answer, and it scarcely needed words to express it. . . .

All the same, in the study afterwards, when her companion went away to count napkins or put some question to the butler, she was explicit and unflinching about her disposition of her income.

"*Damn* your income!" said her fiancé. "I don't care *what* you do with it. . . ."

But of course after they were married they had quite enough to live on. He would join the Government—and try to make it a better Government; she—till babies came—would pursue her special studies in medicine and anatomy.

Lady Medmenham, I hear, proposes to spend much of her money on hospitals and educational institutes for bakers and agricultural laborers; but she is also reserving sufficient funds for her children's futures; and she intends to place at the disposal of competent persons the necessary capital for the complete exposition of the Pituitary Gland, its purport and pretensions, and its immense influence on the welfare of the human race.

THE CHALK-PIT

MY friend Vicars was staying with me at the beginning of August last year. His wife had gone into the western Midlands to visit her relations, and was to rejoin him here early in the next week. It was a Saturday morning—what were we to do? My wife was busy with household things. Vicars was bored by motoring, did too much of that in France; besides, we had all three to go to a garden-party in the afternoon. "Come with me for a bicycle ride," I said firmly. "We haven't bicycled together since 1897, when you had a 'Grand Modèle de Luxe,' which you had bought in France, and which you had to clean fastidiously after every ride. I have got two bicycles. You shall ride one, I the other. We won't go far, but I will take you to see some rather pretty country."

He sulkily assented. But it was a fine day, and as we wheeled along, up shady lanes, under heavy foliage, his natural cheeriness reasserted itself. We passed through the belt of woodland, skirted an opulent farmstead and its suburb of gipsy wagons gaudily painted and drawn up on the greensward on either side of the chalky road. We reached the open downs, and the road ceased to be rideable for people anxious to avoid a bicycle accident; so we got off and walked, and stopped ever and again to enjoy the view over the Channel, with the obnoxious seaside towns reduced to insignificance and the comely downs laid bare for miles and miles, with their wooded valleys, their cornfields being harvested, their villages, and isolated farmsteads.

Vicars, on one of the summits, shuddered at the obvious signs of a yesterday's picnic: strewn newspapers, empty bottles, the gaily coloured cardboard receptacles of cigarettes. "Yes," I said, "disgusting, isn't it, in spite of the view? But here we turn to the left. I am going to show you something the ordinary tourist never comes to see."

We turned the bicycles to the left and pushed them along a descending path on the furrowed side of a flowering down. Thus we dipped till the path became a narrow road which left the open country to enter a wood of rather stately trees. On the right hand the ground sloped steeply through the great tree-stems to a broad, marshy space, the former bed of a vanished river. Here cattle were feeding on the lush grass, and behind them rose another eminence set with larch and oaks, beech and chestnut, till it shut out the northern sky.

But the goal of our adventure lay to the left hand, though still invisible. I turned my bicycle abruptly in that direction and pushed it up a narrow path between the trunks. Presently the trees fell away to either side, and we were at the base of a noble chalk cliff. Two long peninsulas of chalk detritus sloped down on either side, much overgrown with flowery weeds. They completely shut out out the scenery, and left us contemplating the precipitous semicircle of the chalk escarpment. The floor of the pit was flat and smooth, except on either side,

THE CHALK-PIT

where the encircling peninsulas of fallen fragments had built up a garden of wild flowers, especially the dark blue larkspur.

We put our cycles against the sheer wall of the cliff and sat down amongst the flowers. "Now," I said, "here was where the remains were found last year."

"What remains?"

"I'll tell you."

"When we first came to live in this neighbourhood, sixteen years ago, the house and about four or five acres of land up above—you can't see any of it from here—were tenanted by a rather extraordinary man—Reinertz, a South African. He had become very rich in the years which preceded the War, and died more than a year ago, just when the Peace with Germany was signed. He didn't die here; it was at his house in London. During the War he was mostly out in South Africa, but got ill or injured, and died soon after he returned. His widow recently sold this place back to the Duke. . . .

"He was rather a rough sort of chap—I should think—in the beginning of things. I met him out in South Africa first, when I went to see Rhodes at Kimberley—1890, of course—rough and yet not disagreeable. Silent, with far-sighted eyes, clean, and, when he was on the veldt, picturesquely dressed, as they used to be in those distant days. I remember then hearing he had become more settled by meeting an English girl—an ex-governess whom he had befriended at Kimberley. Then again I met him at Cape Town in 1893. . . .

"But this is the extraordinary thing. In 1905 I was

on a holiday hereabouts, looking for a house to settle down in. I forget where you were then—Madeira?—Kamchatka?—— I rode all over this country on a bicycle, and I came up against the Reinertzes' house above this cliff—I'll take you round that way another day. It looked a lovely spot—a very old farmhouse; but they had done it up, enlarged it, drained it, electrified it, developed the garden, made it a bit of paradise; and the whole thing burst on you as a complete surprise. Of course, you didn't reach it this way. You took quite a different road—one which ran out from the station, up the hill.

"Well, not having the faintest idea who owned or occupied the house, I put my cycle against the garden hedge and walked up the garden path. It was in June. The flowers on either side of the path were lovely. I have seldom seen so much colour packed into a small space.

"The front door under an old timber porch was open, and I saw standing in it an evil-looking man. He carried my thoughts back to South Africa. Just one of the types I had seen haunting Kimberley and Johannesburg—Russian, Austrian, German Jew, at a guess. He looked me up and down rather insolently. Presently he was joined by Reinertz—as I gradually realized it was, in my utter astonishment. . . . Are you listening?"

"No. But go on till you're tired, so long as we aren't late for lunch. This is a delicious spot—and in the shade. . . ."

"Well, I will spare you my astonishment at finding

ensconced in a hidden nook of this—then delicious—country, two very pronounced South Africans. I reintroduced myself to Reinertz, but he seemed embarrassed, worried, and preoccupied. However, he dealt summarily and negatively with my question whether he ever let the house, and I had no excuse for remaining, so I bicycled away.

"Three years afterwards we had completed the repairs and extensions in our present home, and I had explored the neighbourhood on the veteran bicycle you have been riding to-day. . . . You will remember that I had to go out several times to West Africa, in between these country solaces. . . . *Do* listen! . . ."

"I *am* listening, out of politeness; but quicken your pace."

"I began to remember about the Reinertzes. I remarked one day that we had been settled here for some three years, and Mrs. Reinertz had never called. Mister was away in South Africa, report said. By a coincidence my wife met Mrs. Reinertz soon afterwards at a great charity bazaar, went up and spoke to her (she was selling South African embroideries), saying I had known her husband a good many years before, out in South Africa—Cecil Rhodes—and so forth. And so, a few days afterwards, Mrs. Reinertz left cards. . . . We returned her call, but she was out. . . . So *that* did not lead us far. . . . I asked, however, to see the garden, which was looking lovelier than ever; and I walked uphill over rough turf beyond the tennis ground, till I came to a low fence of hewn timber at the edge of a great precipitous descent of chalk. This pit below (explained the maid, who knew us) also belonged to Mr. Reinertz, who had purchased it from the Duke. There were steps leading down into it, and it had been made a pleasure garden.

"The Reinertzes, we understood, had a family of five children. The eldest of their boys was at Sandhurst, going into the Army. One of their girls was probably going to marry a young local celebrity. . . . Mr. Reinertz was often out in South Africa, and when at home lived here very quietly, or was up in London, deep in South African business.

"The maid, who gave much of this information, seemed a little ashamed of her loquacity, only to be excused by her father being our milkman. . . .

"I told you that the property after his death was resold to the Duke, to whom it originally belonged. Their eldest son was killed in the War, and the mother seemed to take a dislike to this place, lovely as it was. Last autumn the Duke's agent sent a squad of men to do something to the chalk-pit. The garden above had got out of repair and there had been some falls of chalk. Well, what do you think?"

"Don't know, I'm sure——"

"In clearing away part of the wild garden against the cliff side, they found the remains of quicklime and in it some vestiges of human bone—and some buttons; and one of the buttons had on it the name of a tailor in Trieste. . . ."

"Well?"

"Well, I believe the man I saw in the porch when I

called was pushed over the edge of the chalk-pit by Reinertz in desperation. I believe he knew something about illicit diamond-buying, or similar tricks on Reinertz's part, in his younger days, and had tracked him down to this retreat in an English county. Reinertz, I think, had become desperate and acted desperately. When he looked over the edge of the cliff, and saw the crumpled figure below, he must have rushed down by the roundabout path and managed to hide the body, in order to gain time whilst he got quicklime. . . . Then I can see him, after a while, arranging with the Duke's agent to buy the disused chalk-pit below his garden, and adapting it as a picturesque addition to his premises. . . . And then the miserable mental torture of suspense—extending over months—scanning paragraphs in South African papers. . . . He decides at last to return to South Africa. That, we know, he did. He heard there hardly any reference to the blackmailer. . . . Vague suggestions that 'Old Mo' had either stopped in Austria or got imprisoned or pogrommed in Russia. . . .

"In South Africa we know that Reinertz had some further wonderful good fortune—in diamonds or gold—or something; for he came back to England in 1913, almost historically. People here wondered he did not go in for Parliament, or acquire some public honour by subscribing to party funds.

"Then the Great War broke out, and the carking uneasiness of his undiscovered crime drove him back to South Africa. . . . And when he finally returned to England it was only to die of pneumonia.

"Now, let's cycle home again, in time for lunch. . . . But if you are thinking of preparing a home in England against your retirement, you might, before you leave, go and look at the Reinertzes' place. You needn't buy the chalk-pit as well. At any rate the quicklime has done its work, and I'll make you a present of the tell-tale trouser button."

THE YOUNG MESSIAH

THE Twistinghazers—a fairly common Sussex name—had a very pretty place in what was, fifteen or sixteen years ago, a truly lovely part of Sussex. This was before motor buses and chairs-à-bancs, motor bikes and side-cars, became common; and the abnormal increase of gypsies (who fired the heather and conveyed the primroses in spring to the Brighton markets) resulted in the uglifying of all Sussex outside the gates of strictly private, well-guarded properties.

Sir Channing Twistinghazer was on the Stock Exchange, but loftily and respectably. His grandfather—as you must remember—had been a much-respected person in the City far back in the nineteenth century. He had come from Sussex, or he could not have had this surname, but in those days somewhat playfully lived at Brighton when not in Portman Square and the City; and it was his son, who had much to do with financing the Brighton and South Coast Railway, who bought a derelict great house near Storrington and made it the lovely place you now behold. His son, Sir Channing of to-day, was educated at Eton and Oxford, and at twenty-seven married Lady Sibella, one of the five daughters of the Earl and Countess of Cuckfield. [The Cuckfields had come into prominence a hundred years ago as baronets of a decidedly literary turn, and some influence on

House of Commons reform. Queen Victoria made the Baronet of 1840 a Baron, and in 1859 an Earl.]

Lady Sibella was the eldest of the second peer's daughters. She must have been about twenty-three when she married Mr. Twistinghazer in 1900. Her parents had decided, without communicating the fact to her, that she was rather an ass, and that it would be a capital plan to marry her off to young Twistinghazer, whom they knew as a very well-to-do person in the highest circles of the Stock Exchange, only touching gilt-edged securities and international loans at 4 per cent.

Twistinghazer's father was a widower, and had been knighted ten years before, when the Brighton line had decided to run through expresses to the Isle of Wight without stopping at Sutton. It was generally understood that when his only son, Channing, married Lady Sibella he would give up to them Storrington Park, and would prefer to live at his beautiful town house on the Chelsea Embankment, where (it was rumored among those who were not invited to his soirées that) he solaced his widower's loneliness with the society of peccable ladies. Channing and Sibella would be able to afford, in addition to the house and seventy acres near Storrington, a flat in Ashby Gardens, near Victoria Street; and "naughty Papa," as Sibella came to call her rubicund father-in-law, could have unfettered ease and excessively good cooking within five minutes' drive of Grosvenor Road Station.

However, as good living, a seat in Parliament, the society of painted ladies, and participation in the affairs of a very important railway company unitedly tell on even a robust constitution, it requies no apology to remind you—we forget these things so soon—that Sir Rickett Twistinghazer died suddenly at the age of sixty-nine on the 4th of August, 1914, in the precincts of the House of Commons, after hearing Sir Edward Grey's war speech and realizing its possible effect on the Brighton Company's service between Newhaven and Dieppe.

His son did not succeed him in railway direction, but he had become a power on the Stock Exchange, and helped the Government in such a noteworthy manner in the autumn of 1914 that at the following New Year he was made a Baronet.

Lady Sibella had been avowedly romantic, visionary, and spiritual from the age of nineteen onwards. In appearance she was a little too aquiline to suit a youthful style of beauty, though it was a type of face which might provide distinction and furnish a striking picture in old age. Her eyes were a pale greenish-grey, with small pupils; the tip and aquiline middle of her nose grew a little red under excitement; her teeth required many visits to a firm of dental surgeons when she ceased to bear children. Her hair, originally whity-brown, did not give her face a fine setting till quite recently, when it became a uniform greyish white. She was rather tall; her hands were well shaped, but with fingers a little too pointed.

This seems a slightly unkind description. She did not make on you a disagreeable impression in totality. She was not really an ass, as her father described her in nocturnal dialogues with her mother: she was emotional, as under-educated for her station in life as all the women of her period were, save an occasional Agneta Ramsay, Beatrice Potter, or Blanche Smith; and over and above this, *tant soit peu poseuse*. In an earlier generation she would have been intensely religious—High Church, Low Church, Roman Catholic, or Catholic Apostolic. But she came into the world and grew up when the belief and interest in the old dogmas had faded, when they failed to satisfy or convince even under-educated people, who through the newspapers were aware of the size and circumference of the earth, the course of the Congo, the height of the Himalayas, and the fact that it would take you two hundred and fifty-two years, or a little more, to reach the corona of the sun if you flew thither at the rate of a thousand miles a day. She could not be satisfied with conventional, old-fashioned, seventeenth-century religion; but she yearned for a new revelation. The old was at an end: it had led us thus far, to the triumphs of steam, the use of electricity, religious toleration, county councils, House of Commons government, and the discovery of radium.

"Now we pause for a fresh—a fresh——" she said hesitatingly, in the autumn of 1914. . . .

"Eye-opener?" suggested her brother Charles, when she hesitated for the right word.

"Well, that sounds too coarse. . . . But you know what I mean, and that I *hate* jesting about such matters. I have thought—and *thought*—about this. . . . Before I was married, even, and asked myself whether I—might—not—be—the—the—well, the source of a new revelation. Why—don't be profane and *don't* kick up that rug. It's a carpet from a Persian mosque. . . . Why might not *I* have given birth to—to the New Messiah?

Wilfrid? He has an angelic face, and there has always been *something* in the boy's manner that seemed—you know what I mean? . . .

"I'm hanged if I do. My advice is: put all this rubbish out of your head and send him to a good public school. How old is he?"

"He's nearly thirteen."

"Well, he's better looking than little Channing or Sibby—or Tooticums. That's the only difference *I* can see. Ugh! how my arm hurts. Damnable! The time these wounds take to heal. . . ."

Wilfrid Twistinghazer was undoubtedly a boy with a taking face. His father was a large, comely man, but rather pompous. He could be matched by at least a hundred examples culled from among City directors, Stock Exchange magnates, hall porters, and sheriffs—a stage or two in advance of "John Bull," who was the City man of a hundred years ago. Wilfrid's mother we have already glanced at—not pretty, never would be, but might grow to be distinguished looking. And Wilfrid's brother and sisters, three in number, were just the rather snub-nosed, full-cheeked, clear-skinned boy and girls of a healthy, well-fed English family.

But about Wilfrid there was an indefinable look, a something not easily described, his mother thought. She was increasingly haunted by the idea of having given birth to the New Messiah—some one who should carry on the Divine work another stage farther. But the thought was so awe-striking, so aloof from the trend of Society talk and the ordinary topics of conversation at house-parties, that she ceased to discuss it. Wilfrid was not an effeminate boy; but he was too good to live, most people said, after hearing her description; for the enthusiasm of a mother for her child is not fully shared, save by her unmarried sister or the child's old nurse.

We first saw him when he was about fourteen. It was in the anxious hazardous July of 1915. We had bicycled across the downs to Storrington Park in a month of very uncertain weather. Lady Sibella had not liked to call it a garden party, because—well, no one was giving parties just then; it was simply the assembly of a few friends anxious to meet within her domain a garrulous Under Secretary and a silent Secretary of State, and see if from them could be gathered any information reserved from the columns of the *Times*—a futile quest, as you may imagine. Wilfrid was there, reading with a holiday tutor.

He had expressed himself long before as quite ready to go to a public school. All one doubted was whether, as a possible budding Messiah (for these attributes in a fond mother's mind always emerge into open knowledge), his life would be *safe* at any *great* school, at any *boarding*-school. That, however, was the doubts I instilled into the mind of Lady Sibella when she deigned to consult me in the zigzag paths of her rosary. [She never could quite distinguish between me and my brother, the architect. She asks *him* soul-searching questions about the subject-peoples and the heart of Africa, and sounds *me* on the structure of Storrington Church. But as my brother understands African problems with peculiar enlightenment, and I have very decided views about English architecture, the result is sufficiently cogent to satisfy her vague sense of what is right and proper.]

As the result of my advice—perchance—she decided to send Wilfrid to a famous grammar school in Westminster, where grammar has not been taught for half a century since the school was modernised and made wholly democratic and utilitarian. If he passed through St. Peter's School and developed Messianic features as he progressed, he might straight away, at the age of eighteen or nineteen, make his début at the Stock Exchange, with a flail or some symbolical form of cat-o'-nine-tails, and start then and there his awakening of Great Britain without wasting time on Oxford or Cambridge. Or, if his assumption of the rôle was to be reserved to riper years, he could pass from St. Peter's to either of these Universities, and there condescend to work for a degree. A Messiah who was an M.A. or even a D.D. might be in the preordained scheme of development better suited to the twentieth century.

I had further suggested to Lady Sibella that Messianic principles would, in the evolution of the human race, be more aptly promulgated by one who was skilled in surgery or medicine. The idea appealed to her.

"I *see;* miracles of healing. . . . *Of* course. . . ."

Then she had to move towards the tea-tables and preside over the administration of refreshments. But Wilfrid went to St. Peter's in the next term, and Lady Sibella lived much thereafter at the Chelsea Embankment house to make a home for him in between school hours.

Her other children occupied her thoughts much less.

They seemed so decidedly normal that she did not notice Channing's second teeth were coming irregularly in front and jostling one another into prominence; that Sibella junior was developing face freckles to an unsightly degree; and that Tootsy (Evadne) was becoming fretful at the continuance of her baby name, and was getting into the habit of biting her nails. She did not observe these things till Wilfrid did, in the summer holidays of 1916. Then measures were taken to save Evadne's finger-tips and restore their proper outline, to free Sibella's complexion from any fleck or stain, and Channy's smile from dental irregularity. . . . And Wilfrid did it all, so pleasantly—I was told. The children thought *they* had held up for remedy their own defects. Every one agreed it was a great lark, fussing about teeth and complexions and ladylike hands in the middle of the holidays. And Wilfrid put himself among the invalids by spraining his ankle, bicycling back from Horsham with Sibby's face cream, so that he had his share of the local doctor.

The next summer—and what a summer it was, too, in 1917!—*what* weather and *what* despair about the War!—Wilfrid carried off such a lot of prizes and exhibitions from his school that his mother and, by this time, his father were embarrassed, feeling they ought to give a donation to the school funds. In 1918 he became head of the school, and had to make a speech to the King, when His Majesty, out of old custom, attended the December prize-giving.

Then in 1919 he began to prepare for Cambridge, and in 1920 he became an undergraduate there.

When he was not at Cambridge and not holiday-making in Sussex, he went to various hospitals in London to see "cases," and he became a worker at the Zoological Gardens' Prosectorium. Here and elsewhere he sought for ductless glands, for wonder-working ligaments, for duplicated cæcum, or a nodule in the ear-couch. Early in the last summer (1922), by one operation (under chloroform) on the muscles of the chimpanzi's lower jaw he was thought to have given the creature, when it recovered, the power of uttering articulate sounds, simple words of simple syllables. At any rate it was able to say with emphasis, "Kek!" when it turned away in disgust from untempting rolls of bread. He had become so clever at dealing with and healing local cuts, bruises, strains, sprains, and house-maid's knees among the country folk, that his talent and good nature attracted too large a proportion of Sussex labourers, gamekeepers, and harvesters to the servants' quarters at Storrington Park, and his mother had to remind him of the jealous need of panel doctors and recent enactments in regard to the public health.

His father viewed all this development with some anxiety. Of course, the boy would not need actually to work for his living. He could endow him now with twenty or thirty thousand pounds and leave him a lot more at his own death, and still provide his widow with enough to live on, the girls with good dowries, and a sufficient income for little Channing, who fortunately showed a pleasant aptitude for the City and the Stock Exchange. . . . Hang it all! He didn't want his eldest boy to be an accoucheur or an ear doctor. . . . He ought to go into Parliament. . . . Be Prime Minister—that was his line.

His mother by this time found everything Wilfrid did to be right. . . . The boy—we thought—must have been of exceptionally good stuff not to be spoilt by her adoration. . . .

Wilfrid would have been twenty-one on the 15th of October, 1922. Great preparations were being made (rather against his will) to celebrate his majority. October was a very suitable month—Sir Channing thought—for the gentry to be born in. It placed your birthday at a time when town claims lay dormant and pheasant-shooting began, and when you were naturally at your country seat.

Lady Sibella had convoked a small party to meet Wilfrid at Storrington on the 15th of October. The party included one or two very pretty girls, well born, and with at any rate a little money. Wilfrid hitherto had given no indication of whether his heavenly mission permitted marriage—still. . . .

On the 11th of October his mother had a brief note from him: "A large female tiger has died at the Zoo, and the Prosector is giving it to me to dissect. It promises to be most interesting. I shall stay up to work at it till the day before my birthday. I promise faithfully to be down at Storrington by the 14th."

He arrived, however, on the 13th—but looking strangely ill. The day before he had been searching the carcass for a ductless gland, not always present in the cats. The probe or scalpel had slipped—a slight scratch

THE YOUNG MESSIAH

on his wrist—blood-poisoning had set in. . . . Yet he packed, or had the packing done by a footman, and hurried home to his mother's arms. Doctors were summoned in haste and agony of mind. . . . Wilfrid, apologising for all the trouble he was giving, died with a smile on his face on the morning, the very early morning, of his birthday. . . .

I am wondering whether Lady Sibella will ever recover —ever be near normality again.

MRS. DOUBLEDAY

FELICIA DOUBLEDAY, born Felicia Chuckston, and mostly called "Felisher" or "Felly" in the early years of her life, was first made conscious of some lack of harmony or distinction in her surname when she reached the age of seven. Then the eldest girl next door referred—reflecting her papa's opinion—very disparagingly to the name. Her own—Halliwell—was far superior, prettier in sound, and probably derived from "Holy Well," whereat the founder of the clan had been baptized. Felicia had to admit this and much else. It added to her growing dislike of her father.

In the first place, the flippant-sounding surname came from him, not from her mother, who had once, thirteen years earlier, been known as Bessie Arkwright. Mother, she gathered, had been a cut, or more than a cut, above Father. When you are aged seven, your years of backward memory scarcely exceed three to three and a half. Felly could definitely remember that three years ago things in their home seemed brighter than they were to-day—Father was then in regular work, Mother was understood still to have leisure and a best dress in which to pay calls or attend occasional afternoon parties. Farther back still, thirteen years ago, Mother (she was told) had been a governess in a well-to-do family, and Father at that time was a young piano-tuner of taking presence, a nice moustache, and well-kept hands. Mother was thought even then to have stooped to good looks, because in those days the tuning of pianos was not quite on a social level with teaching. The pursuit had not developed, as it has now, into a scientific and technical section of the Musical career; it was largely a matter of ear and bunkum, the effective use of a screw-driver, a dubious trade in bad music and second-hand pianos, and life behind a brass plate in a suburban or a shabby quarter of the town.

Something had happened to Father two years ago, as to which she knew little or nothing. He had been withdrawn from their home for more than six months, and during this period her mother had worked till she grew old in appearance and ill, thin and with a hunted look in her eyes, but had nevertheless kept the home going, with the help of her two elder children, Elsie and Jeffrey, who were marvels of industry and adroitness, although only aged twelve and eleven. Next to Jeffry came Alice, who was nine, and then Felicia, who was nearly eight, and Egbert, who was five.

This was in 1890. What had led to her father's sentence to six months' imprisonment in 1888, Felicia never knew with any definiteness, partly because she never cared to inquire. It was currently believed that it had to do with betting and horse races. Piano-tuning in Birmingham in the last years of the nineteenth century was on the decline in interest and brightness.

Lablache Chuckston had taken over a rather good business from his father, but after the father's death there was a falling-off in custom, and latterly the younger man had lived principally on his capital, till there opened before him some secretly developed career bringing in very profitable results. This had suddenly landed him in proceedings at the County Court.

When he returned home from his seclusion it was to find a work-shattered wife, estranged neighbours, a broken career. Six months in jail, however, had done him good, physically. The comparatively meagre diet had checked tendencies to fat or to rheumatism. Long hours of lonely meditation had sorted his thoughts and inspired his thinking powers. Before his release he had planned out a new mode of life which he henceforth followed from the age of thirty-nine. It was possibly less moral; it was certainly more daring than his betting transactions, but it need not concern us further, since it has little to do with the story.

Felly had grown to dislike her father; later on she came to despise her mother; she realized her brothers and sisters were hefty, and likely to fend for themselves, but they did not interest her. At the age of fifteen she took stock of herself in the damaged looking-glass of the poorly furnished bedroom which she shared with Elsie and Alice. She was still a growing girl, lanky, thin, and awkward; but there were hints in her face of dawning good looks—abundant dark brown hair, dark brown eyes with long lashes, a well-shaped mouth, and a nose which, if still turned up, promised the development of a bridge. Her teeth were good and she had, at the instigation of a

MRS. DOUBLEDAY

board-school mistress, started a tooth-brush drill. Elsie's front teeth were already menaced by decay, and Alice's were set irregularly.

This board-school mistress was one of the early pioneers in a great movement which Education was starting in the lower middle class. She arrived too late to exercise her influence on Elsie and Alice, but Felicia profited from it in full. She bestowed on the girls in her class all the attention she could give as to their health and their good looks, and taking a great interest in Felicia she enabled her to extend her education beyond the primary course which closed at the age of fourteen—the limit of Elsie's and Alice's schooling. . . . By the time Felicia was eighteen she had learnt to use a typewriting machine and to write shorthand.

"This, my dear," said the schoolmistress, "is equivalent to your having gained a dowry. You need never go to the workhouse or to the bad if you can write shorthand. Strive now to write it better and better, and you will always get employment till you grow deaf and paralytic."

She herself was going to be married at the ripe age of thirty-three to a rising schoolmaster. But before she passed into domesticity and oblivion she obtained for Felicia an introduction and recommendation to Mr. Josiah Doubleday, the head of Doubleday's Drapery Stores, which took up a prominent position in the central part of Birmingham. Felicia was tested by some sub-manager of the establishment as to shorthand and spelling, and with three others was passed for employment on a trial engagement of three months, at a salary of £8, 6s. 8d. a month and a free lunch at the restaurant six days a week.

During the three months of her provisional engagement she saw Mr. Doubleday about three times. He looked at her scrutinisingly once, but passed no remark. At the end of the three months she came up before him to sign documents relative to a more permanent engagement. She was now nearly nineteen. She gave her mother about half her salary to meet the cost of board and lodging, spent much of the remainder on her dress, and started a savings-bank book with £1 a month.

She still slept at night at her parents' house in the southern outskirts of Birmingham, but in the autumn of 1901 she was surprised to learn that they contemplated a removal. The eldest boy was taking up a job in Australia (he was twenty-five). Elsie and Alice had both gone out into the world and left home. The only one still in the nest was Egbert, but he was about to leave evening school and take up a junior clerk's position in Birmingham. Mrs. Chuckston asked Felicia to give an eye to him in the great town. Her husband's new business required his presence nearer to the scene of action, so they were moving to Newmarket. . . .

"If you mean share lodgings with him, well, then, I cannot," Felicia said. "He is of a tiresome, awkward age—seventeen to eighteen. I've my own way to make and am not going to play the elder sister to a growing lad. Why don't you take him along with you?"

"Because he's got a good opening here," said her

mother evasively. "And I'm fairly worn out, looking after you all, and want a *rest*."

She was fifty-two; and although life had gone more easily the last two years, she looked exhausted with many years' strivings to keep house for a restless, plotting husband and a growing family. As a matter of fact, she had shrug-shoulder doubts as to the legality or honesty of her husband's business, but regarded life by now with a kind of desperation. She, at least, had done her duty and broken no law. The others must look after themselves. It might be or it might not be wicked to think thus, but she was tired to death of toiling, of living the life of a household drudge. . . . She wanted a little pleasure, rest, interval for contemplation before she became really old. . . .

So she went away to Newmarket and dyed her hair, and Felicia did not see her again, at least not for many years. Egbert was found a lodging and a landlady who was taken with his good looks and promised to look after him. Felicia, relenting, occasionally had him to a midday meal on Sundays, whilst she remained in Birmingham.

But one day, just after her twentieth birthday, the Head of the firm sent for her to take down a letter or two. This done, he paced up and down on the Turkey carpet of his sanctum. . . . "Mrs. Doubleday has asked me to give you an invitation to come out and spend the next week-end at Hatcham," he said, suddenly stopping and fixing his eyes on her face.

Felicia was very much astonished. She had never yet seen Mrs. Doubleday, only knew her by the gossip that circulated among the women employées of the establishment.

"I—I shall be very pleased," she said, mastering her emotion. "How do I get there?"

"Bring your bag or box with you here on Saturday morning, and I will take you out there in my motor," he replied.

Motors were still a rarity, but Mr. Doubleday had been one of the first persons in Birmingham to take to them. Some years before, when his wife's health first began to fail, and his own riches had become almost burdensome, he had moved out from Edgbaston to Hatcham, near Catshill, on the slopes of the Lickey Hills above Barnt Green. Here he had purchased a derelict country mansion (seventeenth to eighteenth century), done it up, modernised it in comfort and convenience. It stood at an elevation of 700 feet, backed with forest and downland, facing south-east. Though he had had a very meagre education, except in arithmetic and drapery, he had an eye for colour, a reverence for eighteenth-century furniture, and unconscious taste in that respect; and the decoration of Hatcham House left little to be desired. There were fifty or sixty acres of woodland behind the house, and the view from its southern windows over a broad valley, through which the Worcester-Birmingham Canal was carried like a river (with a little lake to feed it), was charming and soothing, seen from this secure elevation.

Felicia had only once been to London with a party of scholars, under the guidance of the good schoolmistress, and otherwise her jaunts from Birmingham had been few and had never brought her into real country outside the heart-breaking landscapes of the Potteries. Even here at Catshill, if you looked too persistently to the north-east and had the far sight of youth, you could distinguish an occasional tall chimney, twenty or fifteen miles away. But to Felicia the outlook, the surroundings, were without flaw.

Mrs. Doubleday had a nurse-companion who might have seemed to Felicia "enigmatic," if she had known of such an adjective. She—Mrs. Doubleday—was obviously very unwell, though her health was supposed to be "on the mend," under that system of enforced optimism which is imposed by doctors and nurses (perhaps rightly) on the mortally stricken. She came in on most days to luncheon and afternoon tea, but retired to her own quarters in the early evening. The nurse made an appearance at dinner (not adding any gaiety to the scene); but as regards breakfast, Felicia's was brought into her bedroom—very cosily—by a smiling maid, and Mr. Doubleday presumably breakfasted with his wife or by himself. Felicia saw him from her bedroom window going out for a ride early on the Sunday morning, accompanied by a groom. But when she somewhat timidly entered the library at eleven (no one had suggested her going to church), he was there and seemed pleased to see her.

He showed her some of his recent bargains in pictures and books, and by the time luncheon was ready they were feeling as though they had entered into quite new relations with one another.

This week-end visit was followed by noteworthy changes. Felicia was promoted to be private secretary to the Head of the firm. In this capacity her week-end visits to Hatcham Park became frequent, and were occasionally supplemented by a Wednesday-Thursday stay. And before much of this intimacy had gone on, she had fallen in love with her employer and he even more so with her. . . . His was an easy conquest directly he had executed certain documents assuring her of sufficient means; and then she was not only his private secretary but his mistress. She was, by this time, twenty-two, and Doubleday was nearly forty-eight.

The first Mrs. Doubleday—if I may call her so—had, twenty years before, been one of the employees of the shop. She was in those days an undoubtedly beautiful woman, and the first five years of married life had been happy in a villa with a little garden at Edgbaston. She had two children, but they both died young from infantile maladies; and she herself, after great riches came and they moved out to the Lickey Hills, developed some strange disorder which, in default of any certain diagnosis, they dreaded might be cancer.

Yet it did not come to a crisis and kill her. She remained a perpetual invalid, jealously guarded and tended by a professional nurse, who assumed, when not nursing, the privileges of a lady-companion. Doubleday's later years had been rendered miserable by this protracted illness. Movement, travel, excitement brought on great pain, so his wife had to remain perpetually at Hatcham, only venturing on short drives round the sixty acres when it was fine. Her husband occasionally went away on drapery business to Manchester, Shrewsbury (where they had a branch), Oldham, and London, or even to Paris and Lyons. On his French outings he occasionally yielded with great distaste to the allurements of harpies. But he was innately respectable and a teetotaller, and inwardly loathed women of light morals, who, uninvited, sat on his knee, who smoked, drank spirits disguised as liqueurs and cocktails, and put kohl round their eyes, and dyed their hair strange colours.

Felicia seemed the solution of their problem. After a while she ceased to be Doubleday's private secretary—he engaged a young man instead—and established her as "Mrs. Doubleday" in a charming villa at Malvern, allowing people to imagine that she was the wife or widow of a nephew in whom he was interested. She had her first baby here. It was a beautiful and healthy child, and Doubleday had many a thrill of happiness contemplating it. He established quarters at a sanatorium hard by, and gave out in Birmingham that a threatening of health trouble rendered it advisable that he should run over pretty often (mostly at week-ends) to the Malvern Hills to seek hydropathic treatment.

Three children in all were given to him—two boys and a girl. He always intended to legitimise them so far as it could be done, and will do so if he lives long enough.

But will he? The first Mrs. Doubleday, strange to say, has not died! She was examined by a very clever surgeon of the new school, just before the War broke out. He located definitely the internal tumour—or whatever it was—and removed it, and Mrs. Doubleday recovered at any rate a measure of health, and knew that rarest of pleasures—absence of pain. The nurse-companion was dismissed with a very handsome gratuity. Either Mrs. Doubleday Number One believed in the supposititious nephew, or she was too thankful for a renewed lease of life without pain in the background to care. Felicia moved from Malvern, dressed as a widow, and established herself in a charming cottage at Catshill. Her children amuse the elder Mrs. Doubleday at Hatcham House, and she is quite pleased to regard herself as their aunt. Their uncle and father is now about sixty-five, but does not look it. For the last five years he has led a perfectly happy life.

EDITH STALLIBRASS;
OR THE SIN OF UNSELFISHNESS

EDITH STALLIBRASS was a sort of second cousin of mine, according as I chose to revive or let fall the distant relationship. She was about the same age as myself, although I remember her being fully clad as a moderately fashionable young woman in the later seventies when I was still a gawky boy.

Even in those days she was noted as "unselfish." She had three sisters, one older, two younger than herself. The three all married in due course, one of them having won over Edith's fiancé, whom Edith surrendered and bade marry her sister Yuphy (Euphrosyne). Yuphy cried for three nights running, Edith certainly for two, and the young man went round threatening to shoot himself for a period of twenty-four hours, during which two households in Bayswater were distraught.

This was about 1882. Twenty years afterwards it was amusing to recall these tragic scenes when you dined with Mr. and Mrs. Everard Hopkins (Yuphy's married name)—she so stout and so made up; he so snarly, cynical, and fault-finding.

What I have written conveys a suggestion of priggishness about Edith, which is not what I intended. She was terribly but not consciously self-denying. She had three brothers as well as three sisters, and eventually remained the only member of the Stallibrass family who did not marry; and was at last the only one of them left in the old house of Porchester Gardens to look after Colonel Stallibrass, who did not die till the year 1900, when he was eighty and Edith was forty-one or forty-two.

He had about £43,000 to leave, and he divided his money pretty equally among the seven children, with a slight bias in favour of Edith, who derived about £280 a year from the lump sum left to her. She also inherited his furniture (very ugly, of the late 'fifties and early 'sixties in date), pictures (no bidding at the auction), and the last twenty years of his leasehold. This she insisted on making over to her eldest brother, also a "Colonel Stallibrass."

I think she half hoped that in return they—her brother Gerald and his wife—would invite her to retain her own room and live with them. They had only three children, and the two girls were already engaged. However, they accepted the present of the lease, but did *not* offer her more than occasional hospitality.

Her second brother, Harold, was an artist, an impressionist painter, at the time of his father's death. He had married an absent-minded woman, also a painter, who was so absorbed with her art that she was seldom properly clad, and most improvident in all household matters. Their inheritance of six thousand pounds was a great boon to them. They took a new studio and became post-impressionists; and as the purchasing world was a laggard in artistic growth, for a while their pictures did not sell.

Fat Euphrosyne's husband, fortunately, had made

money at the Law, so, though Edith had done all she could do to keep the peace between them and preserve appearances from becoming a matter of public discussion, she had but little expense in their case; but Amabel, married to a soldier in India, had a large family, mostly at English schools, and a divided allegiance between Indian camps and garrison towns and uncomfortable temporary homes in England. Amabel was the eldest of her sisters, a year or two the senior of Edith.

The youngest sister was Blanche—Blanche Goodenough. Blanche's story ought almost to be told separately. She was of the fatally good-looking type. You might, in the past, have criticised Edith's face in detail, might have summed her up as comely, pleasant-looking, almost pretty, *quite* pretty when she was nineteen; but never at any stage "heart-breaking." No one ever fell madly in love with her. Yuphy was sensuously attractive till she put on flesh (she was observably greedy after the age of thirty). Amabel was a darling, designed to be the mother of at least eight children, but in middle age she looked *so* tired; and she fretted terribly over her love for her husband (*such* a nice fellow), and her love for her eight children (*such* fine children), and her journeys backwards and forwards to and from India, to be with both in turn.

Blanche, after she was eighteen, was dangerously winsome. She had long-lashed, dancing eyes, which sparkled so much with laughter or with tears that you could never quite distinguish the colour of the iris; cheeks faintly tinged with rose, a pretty mouth and small, regular teeth, nut-brown hair with a natural curl, a lovely neck, and a willowy shape.

She accepted foolishly the first man who proposed, and thus at eighteen and a half became engaged to, and at nineteen the wife of, Henry Goodenough, a borough surveyor. What a borough surveyor is, I could not exactly tell you; but I believe it was a well-paid post, though it had no thrill in it, and that as Henry got it at the age of twenty-seven it was probably obtained in those days through jobbery. His father was also a retired colonel, and his mother was grand-daughter of the first Lord Dalston. The eldest child was certainly Henry's, probably also the second. He was doubtful about the third; and after the third, Blanche decided not to have any more, but frankly to enjoy herself whilst good looks and physical well-being lasted.

Her husband had three hundred a year of his own, and if his salary was an annual thousand, then with his wife's money they should have had between them fifteen or sixteen hundred a year. But this provision began to prove insufficient early in the day, even before Blanche's father died in 1900. Somebody, other than her husband, obviously paid for her Riviera dresses, her yachting costumes at Cowes, and her annual Ascot creation.

After Edith had settled down in a little flat near them, she was drawn into the vertigo of their affairs, if only out of concern for the husband, the son, and the two school-girls. But she would not believe any ill of Blanche —very few people would. Even the tradespeople were lenient about her unpaid bills. Blanche never quarrelled;

she only shed tears when people said or hinted unkind things. Again and again her husband's frowns, remonstrances, turned-away back, and stony silences were conjured into grudging amiability by his wife's cajolery. Things never reached a climax and a break; fortunately, because Blanche began to be troubled with flat foot about the age of fifty, and though it was eventually set right and a moderate degree of activity was restored, she was by that time (the end of the War) fifty-five years of age.

Edith however—— But I should mention there was one more of the seven children to be accounted for— Bertram, the youngest. He had passed through Cooper's Hill College and gone out to India as a forester. In India he had married a very nice woman, the daughter of a chaplain, but with no nonsense about her and yet a disposition of loving-kindness. They had, in course of time, four children; but as Bertram was mainly employed in the Himalayas, above 3000 feet, and they were very happy (being both fond of botany), his visits home were few, and they were able to keep their children with them, except the boy, who came home at fourteen to be placed at Haileybury or some such school and visit Aunt Edith occasionally.

She was very kind to him; yet his parents inwardly thought she might have done a little more for him than take him several times to the Zoo and once to a pantomime matinée. It was not till they came home for good, after the War was over, that they realised why she had done so little, and were surprised that she had done so much. She seemed to have scarcely more than a hundred and fifty pounds a year, and to have sold the balance of the securities which once brought it up to over two hundred and eighty. She had a room at a Bayswater boarding house, but for little more than the storage of luggage and a few pieces of furniture. Her time was spent between the homes of her different relations—Christmas and a summer visit to Gerald; Easter with Mr. and Mrs. Everard Hopkins; Whitsun and Michaelmas with the Goodenoughs; and the rest of the year with Amabel (now a widow), or with her children, six of them married.

Bertram at first accused the Great War of having wasted Edith's substance and stolen much of her health; but though she had shown the right and proper concern over all that had happened, it was only on how the War had affected or might have affected her brothers and sisters and their children. In these directions it touched her to the quick. She had long ago trained as a nurse to attend on her father. But she only figured in that capacity at the bedside of a sister, or a brother's or sister's daughter. Two nephews got wounded in the War, and she managed to obtain permission to go over to France to tend one of them. She evinced, however, intense interest in the babies who began to decorate the households of married nephews and nieces. She had assisted to see several of them enter the world, and had become a godmother to almost all.

When Bertram and his wife had really looked around and settled down by 1921, and excess of brotherliness (accumulated during twenty-one years of botanical service

EDITH STALLIBRASS

in India) had worn sufficiently thin to enable him to see the selfishness of Gerald and Marmion, Harold and Esmé, Euphrosyne and Everard, Blanche and Henry, he intervened in Edith's affairs and more or less forcibly took her over into his wife's keeping. By that time she was about sixty-two, very thin and rather shabbily dressed, and her teeth were giving trouble. Her once pretty lips had an ugly twitch; her faded eyes seemed ever looking for some troubled face she might soothe, some caress she might reciprocate. Louisa (Bertram's wife) said it made her heart ache, this epitome of unrequited affection. "The more I see of Englishwomen," she said, "makes me feel that polygamy should be legalised. Every healthy woman between twenty and thirty years of age should know what married love is, even if it does not last. Separation afterwards is less heart-breaking than enforced abstention, the incompletion of a woman's life, the absence of children." But if she had said this in the hearing of Edith it would have shocked her sister-in-law, who was still of a nineteenth-century outlook.

However, the anxiety of Bertram and his wife came, in this autumn of 1922, to a close. Some one mentioned in Edith's hearing—she was staying with Bertram, near Silchester—that that tiresome second girl of the Goodenoughs was laid up with the new type of influenza which closes or almost closes the throat. She had returned with it from Bournemouth, whither she had been to play golf.

Edith, saying nothing, packed hurriedly a necessary outfit and slipped out with her travelling bag to where the motor-bus stopped at "The White Horse;" drove to the station and caught a train up to town, lodged herself at the Goodenoughs' (the young woman's parents were away), nursed the patient till her temperature became normal and her hair came out; then went off to her boardhouse in Connaught Square and died in three days, overcome with the new influenza in a pernicious form.

JAMES MACGEOCHAN
("JIM MAGEEN")

NOT long after the Great War broke out, I found myself commencing a voyage across the Atlantic to New York, instead of going where my eyes were turned, across the Channel to France. I had asked, on the 4th of August, several people (who were too busy or distracted to send an immediate reply) where, in connection with the War, I could be most useful; but I received in the nick of time an invitation from the United States and Canada to come over for the autumn to lecture on the geography and the general causes of the War. So—our own authorities having approved—I went to New York, and eventually (after other engagements were fulfilled) to the region of the Great Lakes.

As an adventure projected from Toronto, I was taken to lecture at a camp of timber-fellers or "lumber-jacks," not far from Lake Huron, where a rich type of forest extends northward from the United States, and where the winter is milder than anywhere else in Eastern Canada. Here forest work can be carried on till the beginning of December.

However, I did not push my adventure so far into the winter as this. I arrived from Toronto toward the end of the Indian summer, in late October. There was still a glittering of gold and scarlet, a sombrer touch of crimson and purple in the foliage of deciduous trees, of the shrubs and brambles, which contrasted vividly with the blue-green, full green, yellow-green, and black-green of the pines, firs, and yews; and here and there a pleasant relief to the verdure was seen in the reddish grey of bared trunks. Added to these colour contrasts were the vistas of blue lake expanse, the silver-grey of a stream, or the deeper grey of rock surfaces.

The camp—or more correctly the long, scattered village of log huts—occupied the sides of a clearing in the forest. The huts were rough but comfortable. There were long vistas, rendered blue and grey with wood smoke and a moist atmosphere, stretching down to the lake shore and up to the mile-away cliffs, or on a level paralled with the lake outline.

There was much rough good humour among the lumber men, who seemed but dimly stirred with the news of War so far away, in the Old World. Yet they were not unwilling to hear me. The formal lecture, I decided inwardly, should not be given, after darkness had fallen —if you could call it darkness—a moon above in a cloudless sky, and the rosy flare of wood fires. Instead of "lecturing," I would sit in a warm greatcoat and a camp-chair, and "talk" about the War, about the conflicting ambitions which had aroused it, about the countries already afflicted by its ravages, about England imminently threatened. Questions should be invited and answers tendered so far as I could shape them.

Some of the lumbermen were Yankees, some were American Irish, others Irishmen born in Ireland, Canadian Scotchmen, and a few were Americanized Scandinavians. The born Yankees had no notion of the geography of France, Belgium, and Germany. . . .

But in my audience there was one man who more particularly attracted my attention, partly because he seemed to have taken special care of my two companions and myself. He was a fine-looking man, six feet, perhaps an inch or two over, but with a well-proportioned figure—about thirty years of age—laughing blue eyes, a long flaxen mustache; roughly shaved; roughly, serviceably dressed in gaitered, belted moleskin trousers, collarless blue shirt, and a dark serge jacket. He was apparently the leader of the camp, and I found afterwards part of his interest in us was not derived from my discourse, but from the fact that we occupied for the night his log hut, and that in a sense he was dispensing hospitality.

Late in November that year I embarked on an American steamer run by a British crew. The first few days were calm, and after the usual hesitancy and fear of being reproved for venturing beyond a passenger's limits, I took to inspecting the ship's machinery and glancing at her engineers. One of these came to the upper regions, out into the pale sunlight and the pleasant air. He had a shock head of hair—very dusty—and a black, smeared face. But as he rubbed off the coal dust and sweat, and his clear, still merry, blue eyes met mine in friendly fashion, I recognized him. "You're the man—the—the —camp leader I saw and lectured to at—at—the lumber camp near Lake Huron?" I said, putting out a hand. . . . He looked at my hand and at his own—so very black—and replied, "Thanks for your greeting, sir. Me hand's not fit to shake; 'tis too dirrty."

"Then why—— How——"

"Well, I'd got to get over to the Old Country to be recruited; ship hands was few; I know quite enough about engineering to be a ship's engineer, and they was willin' enough to take me. So I gets me passage home free and a bit of money for a spree when I come to Liverpool; and there, I'll take the shillin'."

His name seemed curt—"Jim Mageen"—but I found, long afterwards, this rendering was the shortened pronunciation of "James MacGeochan." His birthplace was Castlerock on the north coast of Derry, and he was "Ulster," though he had lived ten years in North America, oscillating between New York, Ottawa, and San Francisco.

We met once or twice more before the ship neared the south coast of Ireland. Then occurred a disagreeable incident about which there was never given a full explanation. At half-past nine in the evening, not many miles from Cork, occurred a loud noise, a jar and a jerk, and the steamer heeled over at a dangerous angle. I was in a drawing-room library on the upper deck, lying on an ottoman, reading; and with the shock I rolled off on to the carpeted floor. Whist-tables and Bridge-players, flirting couples, and other occupants of this saloon were all prostrate and mixed in heaps. The vessel righted herself almost immediately.

Then ensued laughter, questions, and groans from injured passengers and members of the crew; silence: and a request from some officers with a commanding voice that we who were not hurt would proceed to our cabins and go to bed. The ship had stopped in her course.

There was just a quiet lap-lap of water round the vessel's sides. Then the silence was broken by hoots and whistles and snorts; our steamer was taken in tow, the passengers were all relegated to their cabins, and the lights were turned low. The next morning we were being towed up St. George's Channel, and in due course we reached Liverpool, and after a most rigid inspection by police officers were allowed to depart on our respective ends. . . . On the journey up to town a passenger said that a torpedo had been aimed by a submarine at our steamer, but its damage had fortunately been confined to smashing the rudder and breaking the screw propeller.

I was in France at intervals during 1915, but had almost forgotten the incidents of my American lecturing tour in the problems offered by the Senegalese troops. At the beginning of 1918 I commenced a closer acquaintance with the ghastly struggle which our five armies were waging in Belgium and Picardy. The month of February in that year saw me bound for Péronne to recommence lecturing work among the sections of the troops retired for rest and recuperation behind the front line.

What Péronne was like architecturally in times of peace, before the War, I cannot say; but by the end of 1917 it was little more than three or four heaps of ruins on the eastern side of the Somme. The river was crossed by several repaired yet nearly ruined bridges; it circulated in bright blue streams between the main town and its shattered suburbs. As you entered the precincts of the place, notices confronted you ordaining the assumption of gas-masks and warning you of the dangers of open places, although this warning was seldom obeyed in daytime by soldiers or civilians living in the town. Many soldiers were fishing in the river with rod and line. But the troops returning from duty in the firing-line wore masks and helmets and looked business-like.

Some seven Y.M.C.A. men and lecturers were lodged in the gaunt wreck of a house in a street of the upper town. The left half of the eastern side of this house was flanked by a raised, level garden ending in a brick wall and iron railings rising thirty feet above the street below. The other half of this eastern frontage, through war devastation, descended into a mass of rubble and ruin—bricks, stones, plaster. . . .

I was given a tiny bedroom with just room for a narrow bed and a washstand. Much of the window side of the room facing east had been destroyed, and as a substitute for any other protection the weather was kept out by a stretch of American glazed cloth and a window-frame enclosing one precious glass pane through which at night one might gaze at the awful fireworks along the German lines.

From this dreary and at times alarming centre I attempted a few daytime lectures to tired men. But their delivery was most hazardous. Either we lost our way motoring to the prescribed centre for delivery, or the place agreed upon had been blown up before we got there, or the unit supposed to want a lecture had been hurriedly reabsorbed in the fighting army. At the end of a week all my brother lecturers had been sent back to Abbeville or Boulogne except one, who proved to be a supremely useful personage in other capacities. He was an Irish-

Canadian doctor—apparently a clergyman, as well as a doctor in philosophy—versed in medicine, in metaphysics, in gunnery, and I know not what else. . . .

I was myself allowed to stay on because of a knowledge of French, useful for the time to the officer in command or his subordinates. . . . One of these indeed had served under me many years before in Uganda. . . . I was not only allowed to stay, but a soldier recovering from a wound in the ankle was attached to me as a guide, servant, chauffeur, to accompany me on my lecturing excursions. "He also says," added Colonel Brinkhampton, "he's met you before in America."

He came—with a slight limp—in a neat khaki uniform recently renovated, better shaved than when we had met last, moustache clipped, hair smartly cut, the same blue eyes, with a sergeant's stripes on his left arm—"Jim Mageen!"

Just for a moment I could not put a name to the man, though I saw from his friendly face we had met before. Then I realised. It was Jim Mageen, misnamed James MacGeochan.

"Cap'n Summers thought you might like me 'tendin' to you a bit, whilst you're lecchurin', sir? I've had a bullet through me ankle, but I'm feelin' pretty right now —an' if I c'n be of any service——"

Jim Mageen took charge of me from that time till we were both gassed three weeks later. He made life seem quite different to what it had been since I had reached Péronne. Previously I had made my own bed, or left it unmade, to sleep not only in my clothes, but in my thickest greatcoat in a bedroom temperature below the freezing-point. He imparted quite a new atmosphere of fun and excitement to the small party of men living in the battered house. There were the two lecturers (Dr. Mackarness and myself), two Y.M.C.A. men (one of them a Congregational minister and the other an apple-grower of the Midlands, who was a gallant driver of Ford cars), and another wounded N.C.O., who seemed to be the housekeeper and cook of the establishment, responsible for keeping us alive, so far as food was concerned.

Jim Mageen, however, interfered with everything and got on with every one. He improved the drawing capacity of the kitchen chimney, which hitherto had filled the only sitting-room with smoke. We could now do some cooking there. He found—stole from some other quarters (the officers' mess next door)—chimneys for for our lamps, rigged up a bath on the terrace, which I looked at with respect; only, as it meant ablution in the open air in a temperature between 30° and 40° and an off chance of receiving a shot or a shell from an enemy's aeroplane, I never did more than look on it with admiration. He called me in the dismal dark mornings with hot water for shaving, and shaved me when I did not feel up to shaving myself. He looked through the very little clothing I was not wearing, mended holes, and found and sewed on buttons. . . .

After he had been with us four or five days, the eastern sky was fearsomely glorious at night with rosy flame, with grey-white, yellow-white smoke, announcing

JAMES MACGEOCHAN

many shells dropped on wrecked Péronne. Half-wrecked houses near to us on either side were wholly wrecked. . . .

"I thought ye had a cellar here, like the one they've got nex' door . . . ?" he asked one day.

"Yes, there's a cellar below, but I confess I've funked going down there, at night especially. They say it leads to a chamber dug out of the rock, sixty feet below, and my terror is that if we go down there, and shells do strike the house, it'll fall in ruins above us and we shall be shut up in a tomb."

"Well! I'll bet they thought of that some other time, when the Dutchies was here, and made another way out. I'll go down and have a look."

We all went down the next morning. You descended first into a cellar, then pulled up a trap-door and crept cautiously down a corkscrew flight of steps into the darkness. Where the steps ended, there widened out a flat space of a few square feet; but the descent still continued, slithery and sloping, into a more spacious chamber, the floor of which, however, was covered with broken glass. This was probably where German soldiers had solaced themselves with a carouse in safety. We had two candle lanterns with us. . . .

Jim Mageen investigated very carefully, and after a few minutes said, *"We've* found it!" He knelt down before the end of the chamber opposite to the entry, and showed us the air blowing faintly the flame of the exposed candle end. After some discussion we ascended again to the upper dwelling. Jim went in search of a sturdy comrade or two, of picks, and shovels. Then with his companions he descended to the cavern below, while we cooked and ate an attempt at luncheon.

An hour afterwards they came up from underground, triumphant. They had found again and cleared of obstruction a passageway striking upward at an easy slant, and bringing them out—had they cared to emerge completely, only they did not want to attract too much attention—into the rubbish heaps on the lower street level. Evidently, when the Germans occupied the town, they had not only delved deeply into the rocky foundations of the house, so that they had excavated two lower cellars, but out from the last they had made a bolt hole into the street below.

The result of this discovery was that lunch, being finished, and the bombardment of Péronne resumed, we moved our beds and necessary luggage down below into the two deep cellars, where for several nights we slept in soundless peace and with a feeling of safety; for it was highly unlikely that bombs from the air would not only destroy the house above and block egress upward from the cellars, but simultaneously close our short passage below into the yard and street.

I had, however, to leave Péronne and move to a new round of lecturing in the Oise Valley. Jim came with me. He had been lent a small motor which he was able to drive. There was a lull before the storm, except for the sight in the sunlit air of aeroplanes soaring and spying and dropping bombs. A suggestion of real spring had come into the land, and the snowdrops bloomed in all the wooded hollows. One or two days were so lovely and so quiet that I was deluded into the fancy that an Armistice was impending. Thus we reached Sincéry, where for some good reason our car was handed over to some one else, and a general offered to take me on in his car to my next place, Chauny. On our way thither, grotesquely disguised in gas masks, we passed within a mile of the German lines; and either this became apparent or we had blundered into an attack. We found our road cut by a gap, had to get out and walk to the Oise, and across a nearly shattered bridge into Chauny. At this much-damaged but beautiful place the hospital was established in a great ecclesiastical college. Only one surgeon was left, and to him were being brought several cases of gas-poisoning. Anxious to help, I rushed up to assist, with my cumbering gas mask removed. As I worked with Jim to remove the men's putties and other clothing for their treatment, I felt eyes smarting, nose tingling, mouth and throat inflamed: I, too—and Jim also—was "gassed."

At the encampment a mile distant I was treated, but the very air seemed ominous of a German attack. Bombs began to fall and all sorts of horrors took place during the night. The next morning I was sent away to Ham. Jim, when recovered, was to rejoin his regiment. At Ham there was no accommodation in the hospital, and there was the rumour of the coming German advance. The same car, or another, bore me a hundred miles farther to Abbeville and deposited me at the field hospital a mile from the town. Here I stayed till I was sufficiently recovered to set out for England; then, again, complications ensued from the gassing and there were months of invalidism.

However, in the spring of 1919 I was well enough to

return to the body of lecturers serving with the Army of Occupation. I visited Belgium and saw it in the almost hysterical joy of independence and of gratitude to my own country. I went on to Cologne and took up quarters assigned to lecturers, and thence zigzagged about the Rhineland.

One day I was in Cologne, and was told six marriages were to take place in the Cathedral, Cologne citizenesses espousing non-commissioned officers of the British garrison. Among the wedding couples I saw my friend of the previous year and of the Canadian backwoods, "Jim Mageen," far more sprucely uniformed than ever before, espousing a German bride!

"THE REV. D. MACAULAY"

I WAS at Freetown, Sierra Leone, some fifteen years ago. I had been there on many other occasions, from 1882 onwards, but seldom with much time to spare for independent investigations. The brief sojourn was generally made either on the way to the Congo or the Niger or the Cameroons, or back from those wonderlands to England. Either one's mind shot ahead to embrace the great problems of Central Africa, or, if the voyage was on the return, one feared to contract any more malarial fever before reaching the homeland. But as a matter of fact, to the African student the Colony and Protectorate of Sierra Leone teem with interest. The inland scenery of mountains and forest is—notably the amazing forests of the east—of exceptional beauty and interest; the mammalian fauna of chimpanzis, monkeys, bats, cats, lions, leopards, hyenas, civets, scaly manises, and large-eared earth-pigs, little-known duiker bush-buck, hartebeest, and elephant, is rich and curious; the human tribes are of very varied Negro types; and the language families of peculiar, far-reaching relationships. But for the underlying dread of black-water fever, one might spend years in this part of West Africa, find things of amazing beauty, interest, and horror to photograph, an equal variety to paint, and some of the most bewildering and fascinating African problems to study.

Fifteen years ago there were not any hotels in the capital of Sierra Leone suited to the fastidious European. In any case I was fortunate enough, being there on semi-official business, to become the Governor's guest, preparatory to a journey he and I were to make to the north-eastern frontier of the Protectorate.

The day after my arrival in the comparatively cool winter season—the time of spring and blossom in the forests—I went out after breakfast for a saunter. I had known the town from the early 'eighties onward, but, with the exception of railway developments and tramlines, a few large and boisterously flourishing stores, there seemed little that was new or notable. Ramshackle, verandahed dwellings of native tradesmen or citizens jostled brick churches and colleges of incredible, early-nineteenth-century, Queen Adelaide ugliness, or of the Gothic architecture of 1845. The streets and public places were unpaved, dirty, untidy, with orange peel and mango stones, only relieved from utter ugliness by an occasional fine tree or an assemblage of splendid tropical fruits in the front of a shop. The trees which studded the town, more as the unconsidered remains of a tropical forest than as the result of intentional planting, redeemed the straggling city from vulgarity. Here there was a bombax or silk-cotton, there a sterculia, an oil palm, a date or a fan palm, a bamboo of large size, a banyan fig; and about the fronts of many otherwise shameless houses a wealth of flowering creepers—bougainvilleas, combretums, allamandas, and jasmines.

The populace still contained—though the well-dressed, business-like Kru boys corrected the impression—the well-

"THE REV. D. MACAULAY" 63

nigh incredible "S'a Leone" element—the Negro carried to such a position of caricature as is unknown in the West Indies or the United States. These were the descendants of freed slaves of a hundred years earlier. The men were gaunt, loose-limbed, with preposterously ugly faces, like the villainous drawings of George Cruikshank. But they were dressed "to kill," even in the morning hours; with black frock-coats and black trousers, fancy waistcoats of the 'fifties, preposterous silk ties and tie-pins, clumsy, tall chimney-pot hats of the 'sixties, and lavender or lemon kid gloves. The females, the "ladies," wore caricatures of the Paris fashions of the year before, and enormous hats.

Yet here and there one's eye caught with relief the comparative nudity of the heathen "bush-niggers," those that came from the southern forests; or the dignified, voluminous, indigo, or cream-white 'tobes' of the Mohammedans, supplemented by 'tobes,' turbans, red fezes, or neat, white, embroidered caps.

The Mohammedans of Sierra Leone may range in physical type from the Mediterranean Arab and the Nigerian Fula to the Arabised Mandingo (many of whom, though black-skinned, being distinctly good looking), and to the thoroughly Negro Timne, Baga, Mende, and Vai. But even this last section is extraordinarily well-suited by the Mohammedan costume of the Western Sudan—the neat head-covering, the flowing robes of thick home-spun cotton, and the sandalled feet.

Reflecting on the difference of clothing for the right presentation of the Negro—for you never laugh at him dressed as a Mohammedan or in splendid clean nudity as a savage—I drew up before an attractive, well-furnished store with the French flag flying from its mast. Here, seated at the entrance, was a fine-looking man. Difficult at first to say what he was in race. He was dressed like a West African Mohammedan in a wide-sleeved, dark blue tobe of native indigo-dyed cotton. He wore a dark blue turban and a white, embroidered, red-edged garment, known in East Africa as a "kanzu." This showed at the neck and opening of the chest and in tight sleeves below the voluminous folds of the tobe. On his feet were well-fitting, yellow Moorish slippers, but I also observed that he wore socks or stockings over his feet, no doubt to check the bites of mosquitoes and jiggers.

He seemed to be a superior salesman, a manager, even, of the store, sufficiently dignified to be seated at times at the entrance, unless any important customer came to be attended to. I stopped and stared at him with the unconscious insolence one is led to adopt in West Africa. His fine eyes stared back at mine, not insolently, but with quiet independence. I advanced, assumed he must be an Arab, and after cogitating put an aimless, faltering question in Tunisian Arabic. (What I really wanted to know, by degrees, was whether I might make a sketch of him.)

He replied in Arabic so orthodox that I only understood it imperfectly. Then, seeing my dilemma, and guessing at my nationality, he passed on to English, spoken with an Oxford manner and intonation: "Are you interested in me or in the store? It is commonly called 'The French House,' and has a really very good selection of goods from Marseilles. I think I may say——"

Then, noticing my astonished silence, he continued,

"THE REV. D. MACAULAY"

"Monsieur n'est pas français, par exemple? Les Anglais et les Français s'habillent d'une façon si semblable aujourd'hui qu'un Africain peut facilement se tromper. En tout cas, si Monsieur me dirait ce qu'il recherche. . . . "

"No, I'm not French, though I have had much to do with the French. I'm afraid I stared at you rather rudely, because I was startled at hearing—what shall I say?—an Arab?—speak such English English. I should guess that you learnt it in England?"

"You are right. I did. If you are in search of anything, pray walk through the store and inspect our goods."

"Well—er—I don't know that I came to buy anything, and I have a horror of wasting people's time. . . . I hardly dare confess it, but my interest was not awakened by the store—though I see it is the best in Freetown—but by you. Firstly, I thought, 'What a fine-looking Arab,' and secondly, 'Would he sit to me, if I began a sketch?' But I am daunted now by your Oxford manner. Surely you must have learnt English in England?"

"Well, I began to speak it as a child. My father was an Englishman—or, to speak more precisely, a Scotchman—and my mother was a Fula—lady, I might almost say, and not exaggerate—of Timbo. But, as you guess, I *did* proceed to England, and I might even say I perfected my English at Oxford. . . . At the same time, I ought to remember that I am in the employ of the Marseillaise Company, and manager of their store. These are shopping hours, and if you do not wish to patronise us just now, I must keep an eye on trade generally. So—good morning!"

This was clearly a dismissal of impertinent curiosity—expressed more by a hard look which had come into the fine eyes. At any rate, I took it as such, bowed, and turned away. . . .

At lunch soon afterwards at Government House, when we had reached the stage of coffee, sweetmeats, and cigars, I broached the subject to the Governor.

"*That* chap? Of course I know him. So does every one in Freetown. He makes a splendidly business-like manager for the Marseillaise Company, and it must pay them to keep him as a sort of advertisement. . . . The funny thing is, he is said to be the son of an English merchant who traded with Timbo, the Fula town on French territory, not many miles north of our boundaries, among the mountains. As his father did not marry his mother—though she was said to have been a Fula princess—I take it he was born a French subject; at any rate, he is registered as a French subject here."

The Colonial Secretary was at lunch, and he joined in. "Yes; he's a funny chap—speaks perfect English, jolly good French, Mandingo, and Fula. Fula, I s'pose, might really be called his native tongue. Yet they say, though he's now dressed like a Moor, and is—or seems to be—a Mohammedan, his name was once the Reverend D.—I think D. stood for 'David'—the Reverend D. Macaulay. He is certainly registered here as 'Daudi bin Yakuba.' He has only been in charge of the French store for a year. But he is reported to have arrived at Freetown in clerical costume five years ago, and then to have hurried up country to French territory. The Bishop here says he is the son of a man—James Macaulay—who opened up

"THE REV. D. MACAULAY"

trading relations with the far interior in the early 'seventies. Macaulay is supposed to have married, country fashion, or run away with a Fula 'princess' at Timbo—one of the Amiru's sisters or cousins. . . ."

The Governor replied, "I was just entering the Colonial service—about 1879—and came here in that year. A.D.C. to Sir Samuel Rowe. I remember, oddly enough, James Macaulay—a curious man! Rowe used to say he wanted to become a native chief. He had been a friend of Winwood Reade's. . . . He was remarkably well educated for a trader in those days, and had great ideas of opening up Africa. At that time it was very difficult to get through the S'a Leone hinterland. . . . The Timne people and the Limbas offered much opposition. . . . But this man had a way with him—and he had picked up some acquaintance with the languages. Some people said he'd turned Mohammedan, but I don't think he had any religion. However, he brought his son down from Timbo when he was a little boy and put him in the grammar school here, under the Church of England. So I imagine, if this friend of Johnston's is the same son of Macaulay, he must have gone to Oxford to complete his education, and turned Mohammedan afterwards. Does anybody know when his father died? . . ."

Nobody did know or could remember, and the conversation then passed on to the special points of our frontier delimitation project.

But Daudi bin Yakuba remained in my mind. I saw him the next day, and we exchanged a few minutes' talk. Then I went on the up-country journey; saw forests statelier than I had yet beheld, chimpanzis, pythons, naked, brown-skinned, grinning cannibals, picturesquely costumed, decorous-living, cattle-keeping Mohammedans, lofty palms, stag-horn ferns, magnificent flowers, extraordinary fruits; and returned to Freetown to draw up a report and await my steamer.

The rains had not yet broken, there was no particular hurry, the Governor's hospitality was fully patient, so I stayed on at his house, and when my work on the frontier delimitation was finished, I resolved to have it out with Daudi and penetrate his mystery, so far as politeness might go.

I went to the French store and made some unimportant purchases, chiefly native curios. Then I turned to the manager, who stood at the entrance, and said, "I should so much like to have a talk with you before I go. I don't want to do so in your business hours, but the Governor has very kindly said I may invite you to tea with me in my sitting-room at his house, if you can get away at tea-time?"

"The store does not close till six," he replied. "That would be too late for your tea. But I have a better idea. It closes altogether on the Christian Sunday—to-morrow. If you really wish for a talk, come here when you have done your breakfast—unless you want to go to church?—and I will meet you at the store entrance and take you up to where I live. It is a quiet place, and we can have our talk there. Will that do?"

"Thank you. That will suit me very well."

"Then as I live some way out, and as the Governor goes up to his bungalow that day, let me give you lunch,

"THE REV. D. MACAULAY"

and afterwards I will send you back to Government House."

The next day at nine I walked on to the front of the closed store. There I found Daudi talking in Mandingo to some traders from the interior. He waved them aside, however, and called up a dozen negro porters with machillas or travelling hammocks. We severally got in, and the porters started off at a rapid pace uphill to the Waterloo suburb. "On week days we make this journey by rail, but the trains do not run on Sunday mornings; so you will have to revert to the old custom of travel in the nineteenth century." I replied that I did not mind, as it involved less formality than the train journey; and the scenery was interesting, along a road which bore many traces of having been made a hundred years ago.

We turned off it near "Waterloo" village, followed a side road to the west, and stopped outside a fenced compound which had a thatched roof visible behind. The hedge was of euphorbia armed at all points. A few words in Coast English disposed of the Bulom machila carriers. My host opened the Yale lock of a strong wooden door and we entered the compound. . . .

"This, of course, has only been my house for some nine months, since my family has been here, in fact. I have not done much to it, except to make it less easily robbed by burglars."

We stood before a dwelling in "up-country" style, with a huge, thatched roof descending to a man's height over a broad, clean verandah of hardened mud, to the surface of which a coating of asphalt had been applied.

"This is my mother," he continued, as a seemingly old Fula woman with an elaborate coiffure and a decent native dress came out of the building to greet her son. He bent towards her and took her hand; then indicated me by a gesture and proffered explanation in which I took to be Fulfulde speech. She answered my greeting with reserve, and re-entered the house.

"Would you like to see my wives?" he asked, with irony in his look. "I find Englishmen very interested in that side of my household, and greatly thrilled by my using the plural when I refer to them. . . . I have two wives, very nice young Fula women, whom I have brought down from Timbo. . . ."

"Well, the introduction rests with you. Neither polygamy nor Mohammedanism shock me particularly in Africa. I have no opinion to offer to an African as to whether it is more moral to be the husband of one wife than of two, though I should think three wives too many. It is a matter surely for personal adjustment? Some Englishmen are strictly the husbands of one wife; others find it possible to be the lovers of ten or twenty women. We could discuss this some other time. Don't you think it is rather hot, standing in the sun?"

"You rebuke me. I accept the rebuke. Let us come in and make ourselves comfortable."

We entered the dwelling, and the word "comfortable" was not misapplied to the principal sitting-room. It was large, spotlessly clean, and sufficiently lighted from the verandah on either side. There was a broad, matted seat running along each long side of the big room under the windows. These on the west side were of wooden frames and glass panes; on the opposite aspect, to the east, the wooden frames were empty, but could be screened at night by strong shutters. . . .

"You did not build this house, I gather? Whose was it before you came here?"

"A Swedish missionary lived here. He was a good fellow and went up country to the Mende people, and I took the house over. . . . Now it will be an hour before our lunch is ready, and I must go and see to several things. Can you amuse yourself while you are waiting?"

I said I could, if only by looking at the books which lined the wall at either end of the room. Many of them —I judged by their titles—must have been in use at Oxford in older days: Latin poets and historians, the inevitable Horace and Virgil, Latin grammars and dictionaries, and a Greek grammar. There were French as well as English dictionaries; several books dealing with Arabic—the Arabic of Algeria, Egypt, Syria, and the Sudan; and still more recondite works on Fula, Hausa, Temne, and Yoruba. There were a few novels of the late 'nineties, many paper-covered French novels of later date, treatises on African geography and European history in both languages, and, lastly, two long shelves contained theological works in English of the 'eighties and 'nineties, and among them, in gayer bindings, a few noteworthy rationalist books by Cotter Morison, Farrer, and Edward Clodd.

The middle of the room had no furniture, only a large and rather gaudy carpet. After the wait of an hour there entered a pleasant-looking young Fula woman, decently clad—presumably one of the two wives mentioned—who brought in a small table with short legs. This she placed on the carpet in the middle of the room, and then put beside it two large cushions. Next she added a tablecloth and table-napkins, some forks and spoons, and plates of a clumsy native pottery. Another pause, and Daudi came in and informed me the meal was ready. We sat down on the cushions and attacked the meal which consisted of ground-nut soup, followed by a delicious palm-oil stew or "hot-pot," full of good things, and with a foundation of goat's flesh, the meat of delicate young kids without any goat flavour. Then followed a confection of cocoa-nut and milk, and a dessert of oranges, guavas, and mangoes. The meal finished with delicious Arab coffee in little Arab cups held by metal receptacles.

We washed our fingers in a bowl of rose-water, and then began to smoke—I a cigarette, he a narghileh pipe.

"You've given me one of the nicest meals I can remember having in Africa," I said, rendered genial, and reassured by the good food.

"That's pleasant to hear. Now, do you want to know who I am and all about me?"

"If you choose to tell—not otherwise; your luncheon has made me sleepy, and I think what I most wanted to talk about was the Fulas, and perhaps African languages. . . ."

"Well, you know I'm half English—or half Scotch. You have seen my mother, a Fula woman, and what is more, a Fula woman whose forebears have been high chiefs and who thought in going to live with a white man she was marrying into a chief's family. . . . My father was quite a decent sort, though he has rather messed things by engendering me and dying before he could make himself an independent African chieftain. I really think such a thing was in his mind, a heading-up of the Fula kingdom, when both French and English hesitated to grapple with the Fula power. But West Africa sapped him, and he sickened and died eventually, half-way through the 'eighties. . . .

"I was born in 1876. I'm not quite certain about my birthday, but it was some time in June, so I have chosen June 15th as the day. My father died in our house at Timbo when I was ten. He left about ten thousand pounds, which he bequeathd to my mother and me, but we really only secured the property which could be realised at Timbo, about enough to provide an income of two hundred and fifty pounds a year. As to the rest —property in Scotland—well, I was only a boy of ten, living in a 'savage' part of Africa. My mother was one of the 'savages;' she knew a good deal about the Koran, but nothing about the outside world, except a dim story of the great Mohammedan Emperor in 'Roum'—the Sultan of Turkey. The Scottish part of my father's estate was collared by my Scottish relations, who, of course, never recognised my existence. . . .

"The Lamdo of Timbo—the Fula chief or king—was good to me, and my mother was his cousin. The French, moreover, were beginning to court his favour, and were not shocked that a white man had married in country fashion a Fula woman. They assisted him to settle our affairs. . . . And so I grew up. . . .

"I was very ambitious, very proud of being half a white man, half English. I was vaguely Mohammedan —my father cared little or nothing about religion, and did not interfere. But what I wanted at eleven, twelve, thirteen, was *education*. I was forgetting my English and I wanted to see the world. So I induced my mother to come with me to Freetown, to the sea. We had met a travelling missionary, an Englishman, in the Timne country. He was astonished—I remember—to be greeted in English by a Fula boy! He gave me a letter to the College here, and I soon became their prize pupil.

"What they should have trained me for was *business*, but they could think of nothing but the Church. They sent me to Oxford when I was nineteen. . . . For a short time I was violently religious, Church of England. . . ."

"Well, did Oxford cure you?"

"Oxford—and my half-breed's taint, I suppose you would say. Yes; it quite finished off any belief in Christianity, or least in 'dogma,' and finished my desire to enter the Church of England as a clergyman or missionary. I never took my degree, and I never earned the nickname of 'Reverend' which they gave me here on my return. I came to grief over an Englishwoman with whom I fell in love—and everything was dust and ashes. I came back here to my mother—the only good and true woman I have ever known. She asked no questions, but she healed my wounds. I went back to Timbo, changed my costume, renewed my kinship, registered as a French subject, and then went in for trade. There! Now let's talk of something else till the heat grows less, and then I'll send you back to the Governor's House and civilisation!"

Eight years went by. I had two letters from Daudi at Freetown. In the last he said he was moving back to Timbo to take charge of the Marseillaise Company's business there—and then I heard no more. I had other interests and anxieties which occupied my attention, and ceased to think of him. . . .

In 1915 I was a good deal in France. The War Minister of the French Government had appointed me a member of a small committee of specialists to visit and report on the Senegalese in their camps or in the backgrounds of the battle zone. In the course of my travels I found myself at Fréjus in Provence at the beginning of October. The sleepy hot weather had suddenly left us, and a terrible mistral was blowing from the Alps across Provence. Nowhere have I known it so bad as at Fréjus, where nine to ten thousand black, brown, and yellow Senegalese soldiers were camped.

I had a double object in view: not only to draw up my share of the report for the French Ministry of War, but—and the French Government knew and sympathised—to pass these thousands of men in review from all parts of West Africa, from regions even not definitely mapped, where mountains and rivers might exist of which we knew nothing, and examine them as to their languages. I was, as a young French officer remarked, proud of his English slang, "dead nuts" on the study of the semi-Bantu speech forms of Senegambia, and a French ethnologist of our Commission had already signalised two of which I had never heard before.

At Fréjus, after *déjeuner,* an officer said to me, "Things have been pretty bad with us since the mistral began to blow. Three days ago we had a small army encamped here, most of it men who had been in action a month ago. Now, since the mistral found them, six or seven thousand are *hors de combat,* dying of pneumonia and other chest diseases. C'est la fin des Sénégalais!" A junior officer questioned me as to my exact name. I satisfied him that he spelt and pronounced it correctly. "I ask you, because amongst our Senegalese native officers is un drôle de type—fils d'un Anglais—paraît-il—et d'une femme Peulh. He is very ill, but says he knew you once in Sierra Leone. . . ."

I accompanied him to a small tent. Inside, on a narrow bed, under a dark-brown, bristly blanket, lay a tall gaunt man, with glowing eyes, haggard features, and a dull yellow complexion. Already guessing who it was, I bent down and said in English, "Daudi bin Yakuba, this is very sad! After eight years to meet you, and find you so ill!"

With difficulty he found his voice and said, *staccato,* "Yes. . . . This—is—the—end—I think. . . . Goodbye."

And a feverishly hot hand came outside the dark-brown Army blanket and pressed mine. . . .

There were three of us inside the poky little tent, one of the three an irritable Army doctor. I had to withdraw with my guide, and I have never seen "The Rev. D. Macaulay" again.

THE END OF THE DAY

I WAS stranded in London last September, and had to remain there during much of the month, as it pays a centre from which I could pay a few visits and a place in which I could conclude several transactions concerned with study and publication. One of my business visits was to a pale-faced, summer-weary publisher, panting for a holiday in Switzerland, which he could only take when his partner returned; a second or indeed several calls were due to a palaeontologist examining ancient human remains brought from South Africa. He had such anticipations of discovery that he was indifferent to the season of the year and the shocking weather conditions of one of the worst Septembers known within the age of weather records.

But, I, myself, when held in London, was restless, being sufficiently wedded to the country to be always reluctant to spend many days away from woods and fields, downs and streams and forest by-roads wherein one can dream of the England that was in prehistoric times, with a generous fauna and a wealth of wild flowers. Yet even with such prepossessions, London has a more wistful kinship with the past in September than at any other time. You can be seen there without the nuisance of being asked to evening parties or to club dinners, or being inquired into as eccentric if you think out your thoughts through long excursions on the tops of motor buses through terrible sordid or icily respectable suburbs, or past seductive villas hidden in a still luxuriant foliage of chestnuts and limes. I liked the loneliness—in a way. I looked out from the sixth floor over a western segment of London, identified this and that steeple, tower, or minaret and dome, recognised the roof of Buckingham Palace and the gilt angel on the Queen Victoria memorial, the hotels of Piccadilly, the verdure of St. James's Park, the luxuriance of creeper-covered trellis-work which masked the ugly brick backs of stucco-fronted houses. I wandered out to Kew Gardens, revisited the Zoo, rode on the roofs of motor omnibuses to Barking, Willesden, Barnes, and Dulwich. Doubtless there were friends still lurking in London, but they did not interest me and I might not interest them. Whom to go to and take tea with?

Then some allusion in an evening newspaper reminded me of Janet Levy—or "Janet Lavermont," as you might possibly remember her—one of the great actresses of the 'seventies.

I had known her at a later date than her first effulgence, somewhere about 1879, when she must have been over thirty, if she was born in 1847, as she now admits—known her so far as a Royal Academy student in painting just able to afford a dress-circle seat once in a way could know a celebrated actress cut off from the adulation of insignificance by the footlights and a great fame. Thenceforth, whenever I was in England I went to see her act, sometimes twice or thrice in the same piece. At last, in 1885, through the Hepworth-Dixons' tea-parties, I got to know her personally, though slightly. Our acquaintance was much advanced in 1894, and by the end of the century my wife and I had come to know her well.

The name under which she acted between 1867 and—when was her last appearance?—1912 was quite different either to Janet Levy or Janet Lavermont, Lavermont being the surname of her first husband. To quote her stage name here, though it would lead to a great clearing of your brows, and you would say, "*That* woman! Why, I knew her as well as you did!" would nevertheless be a breach of manners and might turn a harmless story into a fragment of biography. There are a few remaining people who knew Lady Hartfelt privately, from the days of her girlhood onwards, through her three marriages to the present day. They will recollect the famous name she acted under, which suggested nothing of the Jewish element in her make-up.

As a matter of fact, her father was only half a Jew (he was a great theatrical florist), and her mother was not Jewish at all. But the dash of the Israelite, though it did not darken her once-golden hair, nor crook her Grecian nose, nor turn the iris of her eyes from blue to brown, gave her something in her looks which was not "English," some spice, some glamour of the East.

Somme toute, it must be admitted she was a beautiful, attractive woman, whose grace and good looks the fashions of the 'sixties, 'seventies, and 'eighties could not mask or render ridiculous. And added to this beauty of face and figure was a wonderful voice, a *mezzo-soprano,* deepening with age into a contralto—literally a voice which wooed you, though, when I first heard it, she was thirty-two. . . .

I, much her junior, fell in love with her when I saw her act in 1879. But I did not meet her off the stage to speak to until 1885, when, blushing and inclined to stammer, I was introduced to her at an afternoon party on the north side of Regent's Park. She was nearly as beautiful off the stage as on; but with no glamour of the footlights you were less surprised at being told she was thirty-seven. There was a slight twinge of melancholy in her contralto voice, and the large eyes had a hint of weariness in their kind gaze. . . .

It was this that endeared her to me most. Whatever she might be—and her sins, if there were any, were those of a goddess—she was *kind*. One felt instinctively she had none of that hard veneer which so many actresses and public women acquire; that business-like manner which only arranges to waste time and smiles and attention on ten thousand a year, at the least. Our introductress told me either before or after the presentation that Mrs. Lavermont was in great stress over private affairs, that she was trying to divorce her worthless husband, but that, as he sedulously avoided committing the actions of assault and conjoint unfaithfulness required by the divorce laws of those days, there she was; she made no progress, and her spouse lived riotously on the money she earned.

In 1894 a change had come over the scene. Either the unfaithful, inappreciative, squandering Lavermont was dead, or a way had been found through the Divorce Court to regain her freedom. She had married again—

I think in 1891—this time a much superior husband—Colonel Horace Travers, I will call him. The name expresses him as well as the one he really bore. He was secretary to an immensely wealthy City company chartered by King Richard III.; he was a Colonel in the Volunteers, very rich, effulgent, good looking, a connoisseur of wines, of music, pictures, and women. He was a widower with three children when he made his second marriage, and had one other child by Janet, whom he left a widow once more when he died in 1901, died from excess of good living.

He had, nevertheless, given her a secure and happy married life of ten years. He would have shrunk with horror and paled with indignation at the idea of getting drunk. He had probably never been drunk, but he had hastened his death at sixty-one by taking for forty years far more liqueurs and rich wines, *pâtés de foie gras,* caviare, dressed crab, prize asparagus, and melted butter than his digestive organs could assimilate and put away without leaving a harmful residue.

I knew also that Janet in 1902 or 1903, though heartbroken at the death of her Horace, had yielded to the importunities of Sir Henry Hartfelt (I will call him), and had married for the third time and established herself and Travers's daughter in a charming house on the Chelsea Embankment. I saw her act (superbly) as the Nurse in *Romeo and Juliet* at Ada Balsome's benefit in (?) 1912. But after that year I was much abroad; then ensued the distraction of the War, and I did not regain my interest in "Janet Lavermont's" existence till the summer of 1922. I was vaguely aware, in the last year of the struggle, that Sir Henry Hartfelt had died, and that Janet must be for the third time a widow.

So I took a taxi one afternoon during a break of sunshine between two days of storm and rain, and drove to Lady Hartfelt's address on the Chelsea Embankment, with the hope of finding her in at tea-time and renewing the lapsed acquaintance. A minute's incertitude in the hall, awaiting the answer to the servant's inquiry on the speaking tube; then, "Lady Hartfelt is in, sir, and will be very pleased to see you. . . ."

The drawing-room was on the first floor, up a handsome, broad staircase of shallow steps. It had a row of tall windows with balconies looking towards the river, and so many tempting bookcases that it may perhaps have been styled the library. But I had little eye and too much good manners for this untimely investigation of the furniture: my gaze at once fell on Lady Hartfelt and on her daughter. The daughter, having been born in 1892, must have been close on thirty. She was capable looking, tailor made, and dressed to go out (I realised, with a hope that she was going).

"It must be ten years since we met," I said to her mother. "Your daughter has changed very little since then." (Was this tactful?) "And you look hardly older, though I suppose, like most of us, you have gone through a lot of terrible things in the interval?"

"Yes! . . . But it is funny your coming to call. . . . I have thought of you several times lately," said Lady Hartfelt, "so much that I ended by thinking *you* must have died, and that I had overlooked the obituary notice in the papers. My dear Henry, as you probably heard, *did* die at the end of the last war year, and his death blotted out for the time everything else. . . . You look to me quite ten years older for the ten years that have passed. I suppose, like most other people, you have been through trouble of some kind?"

"Yes; only health trouble, fortunately. But I haven't come here to talk about anything but you."

"Well, nothing could be more appropriate, because, as it happens, I want to talk about nothing but myself. Gracie has to go out. She is a little ashamed at having to be in London in mid-September, when she ought to be at conferences in Switzerland or Birmingham, so she is going to take tea with Elca Alston, who is also in London on some lame excuse. Perhaps literally, for *I* am laid up with a swollen ankle! Don't quite know what it is, but the doctor has forbidden me to stand about till it is well. That is why—being also seventy-five—I don't get up to receive you!

"But it is *most* nice and opportune, your coming. Gracie can now go with a clear conscience and leave us alone for quite two hours. Tell them to bring tea before you go, dear," she added.

Grace shook hands and went out. We sat for a time almost silent, both looking into the wood fire and perhaps passing in review the happenings in both lives since we had last met. There was a flicker of rain on the windows, which passed away, and pale sunshine returned. The old manservant, divining his mistress's wish, opened one casement to let in the southern air, and arranged the tea-things within her reach so that she could serve tea without difficulty. We were both sufficiently people of the world to help ourselves silently and independently to cakes and bread and butter. . . .

We ate and we drank, and then, taking our eyes off the logs and the leaping flamelets, we looked into each other's faces. . . .

"I can read your thoughts better than I did ten years and twenty years ago. It's rather nice, you know, to have reached an age like mine"—she indicated with her beringed right hand the cream-white wig or transformation which so well became her—"when you can say what you like, express your *real* opinions, and tell the truth about your life. Thank God! I've kept my wits so far, and my memories. I've got enought to live on. My elder children, the Lavermonts—you know—are all provided for, and Gracie's father left her a thousand a year and me two thousand. Then my third husband, darling Henry—you know there *was* a German strain, a hundred years ago and more, and they used to spell the name with a *dt* instead of only a *t*—in fact, I believe the original founder of the house wrote his name 'Herzfeldt.' Why didn't they boldly call themselves 'Heartfield,' if they wanted a change? However, my dear Henry was English, *through and through,* and this terrible War really broke his heart. I remember only in 1912 how he hoped Germany and England were going to come together. *How* hard he worked at that Conference! We gave such a party to them all—all the delegates, I mean—in this house, and took them a trip on the river up to Richmond, where we gave them tea. . . .

"However, as we've got only two hours for our talk,

THE END OF THE DAY

I mustn't digress. . . . What I wanted to tell you was that Henry left me for my life this house and five thousand a year. The rest of his money went to his son by his first wife, and to some nephews who are in the firm—tanneries and artificial manures, you know. . . .

"Have a third cup? Do! Shall I ask you to ring for Jacobs and have a fresh pot made? One ought not to water this China tea. . . .

"Well, now, what I meant to begin by saying was that I have determined, while I have my wits and retain my memories, to write my life as an actress. *Of course,* not to take up the utterly wearisome task of *writing* it all down, myself. That would give me writer's paralysis, and my sight couldn't stand it. . . . But just to sit here by the fire—if it isn't summer—and dictate it all to Gracie. Gracie's a wonderful person! She learnt both shorthand and typewriting at her college, and does all my correspondence now, except here and there *une lettre intime.*

"So! . . . I shall just dictate bit by bit my life to her; and why I thought your coming so *particularly* providential—almost as if I had evoked you from my thoughts—was that you know all about publishers and their wicked ways, and can advise me who to go to. . . .

"I've got *heap* and *heaps* of photos—photos of the 'sixties—every one very small and crowded, incredibly tall chimney-pot hats, and fixed smiles and spread-out skirts, and columns, and curtains, and large volumes heavily bound, and people holding baby croquet mallets in an over-crowded drawing-room, or guns against a drop-scene background. . . . And photos of the 'seventies. . . . Florid, faded, sentimental. . . . Hair fringed in front and dragged back behind, lolloping over the frilled neck; and dresses straight up and down, and you were clothed *literally* from head to heels. . . . Only a little strip of neck showing, and that masked by a ribbon and a locket. . . .

"And then the 'eighties and their crinolettes! And the 'nineties. . . . Not so bad, the 'nineties. . . . And the large shoulder sleeves. . . .

"Here's your third cup.

"I had rather a nice girlhood. My mother had been an actress. I think she was a *dear,* from what I can remember. . . . Probably she had several love disappointments and mishaps, because she must have been very pretty in the 'thirties and 'forties. I dare say she only married father to get a position and an income, though he really wasn't a bad sort—a kind of florist to the theatres—to Covent Garden and the Opera, more especially. Our nurseries were out at Mitcham, when Mitcham was quite the country. . . . I had several brothers and sisters, and as far as I can remember they were all good looking. But all came to grief eventually, in some way or another—mostly in the States.

"Father was half a Jew. His name was Levy. But he wasn't a bad sort at all. . . .

"Racing in some way did for him, and he blew out his brains in 1865, when Something-or-other won the Derby and he had staked everything on Something-else doing so. . . .

"*Poor* mother! All her children, as far as I could learn, wanted to go on the Stage. Owing to father hav-

THE END OF THE DAY

ing so much to do with the flowers for the theatres, we got lots and lots of orders. . . . But the only one, I think, who really entered Stage-land was myself. Mother was reluctant, but I was so pretty, and even as a child I had a good voice. . . . I first appeared in a Drury Lane pantomime when I was eighteen, after father's death. . . . The next year I met *Charles Dickens*. . . . *Think* of it! I wasn't much more than a chorus girl, but he thought I had talent, and he introduced me in 1867 to Marie Wilton, and after that I got on well.

"Then there was a racing friend of father's—my first husband, as he became—Jimmy Lavermont. I believe—now—*he* had something Jewish about him, and that Lavermont was not the name he was born with. . . . He was much younger than father, and had—so they said—a lot of money at one time, and bred race-horses down in Sussex. . . . Well, after I had come out at the Prince of Wales's—only in a small part, but I made it quite a success—*how* I used to work in those days!—he came about me a good deal, was always sending me bouquets and rings. And poor mother was so hard up, and so many other men of the same stamp buzzed about me—well, I went to live with him without getting married—at first—but when I told him later on a baby was coming, he did the right thing—as he phrased it: he married me.

"Two years later, I made a great hit as 'Esther' in *Caste*. And the droll thing was—Marie Wilton was so kind and saw the joke of it all!—the droll thing was, I had my *own real* baby on the stage!

"After that year I never looked back as an actress, but I gradually got more and more into trouble in my home life with Lavermont. His luck in racing came to an end; he got into debt. I had to slave at the theatre to keep things going and provide for my three children. At last, in 1886, things became unbearable. I was sure he was not faithful to me, but as to that I had ceased to care. I didn't see why *I* should slave to keep him, when it was all I could do to earn enough—seven, eight hundred pounds a year—to keep myself, as a lady, educate my children, and be incessantly at work at the theatre.

"I obtained a judicial separation in 1886, and in 1888 I met Horace Travers, who was recently a widower. He fell in love with me and helped me through several tight places. . . .

"In 1890, to my immense relief, Lavermont died; and in the same year, as soon as it was decent, I married dear Horace. In 1892 I left the Stage—as a profession—and Gracie was born.

"From that time onwards I have never had an unhappy hour, except in grief over the death of my husbands. . . . *How* I wish the two last could have met— in life. . . . They would *so* have appreciated one another!!"

"What shall you call your book?—*An Actress's Memoirs?*"

"*Dear* me, no! *Nothing* so banal. I thought of the title first, before I decided to write at all: *The End of the Day*. It *is* the End, alas!—though I may live to eighty or eighty-five. But *how* sad the finality is, is it not?"

Here the sinking sun burst through the rain-clouds and flooded the western side of the windows with yellow

THE END OF THE DAY

light. The sparrows cheeped at the return of cheerfulness. The door opened and Grace Travers entered. We glanced up at her.

"Well, I hope I stayed away long enough for you to have your talk out. I found the tea-party *ra*ther dull. Elca was put out because her brother and his wife are returning from China and want to occupy her best bedrooms! She was very much annoyed!"

THE JEWELS AT DAVENSHAM CASTLE

ABOUT two miles—perhaps a little less—from Davensham station, on a branch line of the Brighton Company, in West Sussex, stands Davensham Castle. It is such a well-known and historically sumptuous building that it is hardly necessary to describe it. It was begun in Norman times, continued and beautified under the Plantagenets, when you really wanted a castle to live in if you wished to live comfortably. It was added to under Henry VIII; then confiscated from its owner—a favourite who had lost favour and was beheaded and died, last of his line, for resenting the king's quarrel with the Pope. It was given in the king's dotage to a young favourite, great-grandson of a Lord Mayor under Richard III; slept in by Queen Elizabeth, had famous revels under James I (at which both the king and queen became tipsy), was besieged by Cromwell, restored by Charles II, and welcomed William III, and, later on, the Protestant Hanoverian dynasty.

Its marquis, late in the reign of George II, was made a duke, for which he had to pay rather heavily. The third duke reigned at Davensham from 1800 to 1825, and was one of those who revelled with the Prince Regent, with whom, however, he alternately quarrelled and posed as a Radical, denying the value of sovereignty and the existence of a Deity. And then he would make it up

JEWELS AT DAVENSHAM CASTLE

with vinous tears, curricle racing, and attendance at the Brighton Pavilion.

The fourth duke, who succeeded in 1825, was pompous, and spent a good deal further of the family's funds on creating a variant of the Protestant Church. The fifth duke was a messer and a muddler, who worked first with one party and then with its opponents; resigned a Ministry under Disraeli and misdirected another under Gladstone; fought feebly against Darwin in now-forgotten literature, and secretly speculated in wild-cat schemes, with some hushed-up failures which added to the growing impoverishment. The sixth duke was really the second son, but was far and away the most sensible of the stock. He went into the Army, served in India first as Somebody's A.D.C., then joined up over a native war; and even after his elder brother died and he succeeded him as Lord Davensham, while he was a colonel in South Africa in the Boer War, he went on fighting in the Transvaal till victory was assured, before he came home and took up his inheritance.

Well, by that time the old Duke of Dulchester was behaving most erratically. He was a widower, but showed alarming signs of wanting to marry again at the age of seventy-five. His children and his daughter-in-law, Lady Davensham, feared to let him out of their sight in daylight in case he tendered a proposal and there was an action afterwards for breach of promise of marriage. They pressed on the marriage of their governess with the vicar, and on her departure engaged a tutor. However, at last he died; and in 1905 the new Duke of Dulchester from that time forth began very thoroughly to look into everything, economise, sell, develop, cut off the bad, and make the good better. There was one direction in which he may have seemed (only very few people knew about it) to interfere with his family's past.

The first duke, when he was a marquis, had commenced almost religiously—being fond of glittering things—a wonderful collection of jewellery. It was guessed that he had expended over £100,000, and that at a time when jewels were sold far more cheaply than they are to-day. The second duke inherited his father's passion for this form of beautiful things; and although the family estates had suffered by making their secret gift towards George II's debts, he must have spent at least £50,000 during his thirty years of dukedom in buying celebrated jewels. He acquired thus Marie Antoinette's emeralds.

The succeeding dukes had to stop, except for an occasional purchase. They had large families, and during the evolution of the nineteenth century the children of dukes required larger and more definite provision for their livelihood; and it was not so easy to thrust them into sinecures or well-paid careers. Besides, during this wonderful period, when man advanced by tremendous strides towards becoming a demigod, this particular ducal family produced a much larger proportion of women than men; and sinecures, well or ill paid, have practically never existed for the female sex. At the same time it was becoming hideously expensive to marry a duke's daughter; so the daughters of the fourth and fifth dukes mostly grew to old or middle age as single women, and some sort of provision had to be made for their maintenance— at least seven hundred a year apiece. A cluster of the fourth duke's daughters lived at Dulchester, and did an infinitude of good amongst the poor and the clergy of its cathedral; the sisters of the sixth duke were still all living at Davensham Castle when their father died in 1905. Their only surviving brother, the duke, had begged them not to turn out of their rooms after their father's death. There were at least thirty presentable bedrooms besides their five, his own and his wife's two, and the nurseries and servants' rooms. His own family was more moderate in number—two boys and three girls; and the two boys were away attending to their careers, and the girls being educated and what not.

But in the month—May—in which my story begins, the duchess, with a daughter or two, was up in town staying with relations, and the duke's sisters were all in their flat in Ashley Gardens for the London season, which they were reviewing discreetly, being in mourning. It was 1906. During the grim twelve months after the old duke's death, the death duties (not so large then, but still formidable), coupled with the revelations that were made of rotten investments, unyielding properties, unlettable houses, worked-out coal-mines, and the stupid inefficiency of the hundred-years-old firm of family solicitors in Lincoln's Inn—the new duke acquired two permanent wrinkles on his forehead, and his abundant hair above it turned grey. But he was in reality intensely happy, trying to save his family from bankruptcy and make them solvent, trying to do this with little or no leakage of knowledge to the general public.

The great London house in Portman Square was let for three years to a South African millionaire at £1,000 a year, which, at any rate, paid for its repairs. His wife, for a year or two, if she had to go to London, willingly used the flat of her sisters-in-law in Ashley Gardens. They—devoted women—touched to the quick at being allowed the retention of their rooms and hospitality at Davensham, not only made room for their brother's wife whenever she had to come to town, but gave up their flat to the duke himself when he required to stay in the metropolis. In short they made common cause with him in the secret family effort towards financial reform and solvency.

The interest of the little group was concentrated more especially on the marvellous collection of jewels stored at the castle and, until its letting, at the town house. These, for a hundred and more years, had been discreetly shown from time to time to trustworthy visitors. It was surmised that the retention of this marvellous collection was, without being specified in any legal document, almost a feature of the dukedom. The late duke had declined many times to sell any item of the collection, even retaining much that was *baroque* and tawdry, especially the crown jewels of seventeenth-century Poland. He had seemingly exacted no pledge of retention from his successor, any more than he had given any undertaking to his own father, the "Evangelist," as he was nicknamed. And the evangelical fourth duke, eager as he had been to spend funds on the support of his church, had not even contributed a cairngorm to the breast-plates he had designed for his clergy. But they had not been afraid of guarded ostentation. All through the nineteenth century the various duchesses and their daughters had gone to

JEWELS AT DAVENSHAM CASTLE 95

drawing-rooms and state balls bedizened with diamonds, pearls, rubies, emeralds, cat's-eyes, peridots, and fire opals, which were afterwards replaced in the iron safes or glass show-cases in Davensham Castle or Dulchester House, Portman Square.

Of course, even in the nineteenth century you could not keep a collection of jewellery worth anything between two and three hundred thousand pounds in a country castle or a London house without some artifice—something in the way of safes and strong-rooms, and chests of drawers with Yale locks for the cairngorms, amethysts, and garnets. But to the enlightened intelligence of the new duke, who had known Johannesburg and Kimberley, this immense wealth, this renowned collection, must be far more efficiently guarded, if it was to be preserved from the burglars of 1906, 1907, 1908.

It might indeed be found, when all was explored, to stand between him and insolvency. His wife was a sensible woman, the daughter of a great Indian judge. She referred to jewellery as "trinkets," and did not aspire to decorate her person with precious stones or the feathers of rare birds. Her mind rose above the level of a South Sea Islander's. Her daughters would be educated to hold the same opinions.

From the beginning of 1906 the duke gave himself up to the study of precious and doubtfully precious stones. Every one thought it natural on the part of the owner of such wonders as Cardinal Gianpetri's rubies, the Balas diamond, the opals of Catherine II, and the three yellow sapphires worn by Lola Montes of Bavaria. He studied jewels in the rough at the Cromwell Road British Museum; in the smooth, the cut, the set, the historic, at the older branch of the British Museum in Bloomsbury. He renewed chance acquaintances with South African pioneers, whom thrilling diamond discoveries had converted from gruff ungrammatical Canadians, South Africans, or German Jews into quite passable citizens of the upper world, baronets, and such-like. He asked down to Sussex reticent Hatton Garden diamond merchants, with German, Dutch, or Israelitish names, to inspect his marvellous jewels and tender advice as to resetting, or venture on an appraisement of value.

These activities continued for quite three years, in the course of which the death duties were paid off, the unprofitable property was sold or let for more suitable ends. The South African millionaire bought Dulchester House, Portman Square, for £100,000, and the duke acquired, renovated, and furnished for half that sum a much smaller but delightful seventeenth-century dwelling in Westminster. He bought three motors and sold all his horses, except one that was past service, and the pony of a governess-cart, and three for riding.

At the beginning of 1910 he now felt free to interest himself in parliamentary affairs, and to look into the fuss that people were making over woman suffrage.

Then occurred the jewel robbery at Davensham.

The duke, when he was at home, often encouraged the neighbouring people to come over on Saturday afternoons and be shown the castle. If he was at home himself he would take them round the showable parts, and would sometimes—if they pressed for it—give them a brief glimpse of the more famous jewels. Under any condi-

JEWELS AT DAVENSHAM CASTLE 97

tion there were show-cases of thick cut-glass in the hall which had in them some remarkable, if not excessively valuable, stones, pebbles, specimens of jade and jet. He had some such party round him on Easter Saturday of that year, when, beside the Sussex holiday-makers of round about, there were several shrewd-looking visitors from London.

At the beginning of June in that year, not long after King Edward's death, a party of wealthy South Africans (so they were said to be) came down to Davensham village in a motor and put up lavishly at the Dulchester Arms—three men and a woman, besides the chauffeur. They motored over on the Saturday to Davensham Castle, and were quite surprised to hear that the duke and duchess were not there; said they had met the duke in London and understood he would be back in time to show them over the castle. . . . What were they to do? They had to leave shortly for South Africa, in fact, would motor on from Davensham to Southampton and take the boat there. . . . Could they not be allowed to glance at the wonderfully interesting hall and the show-cases, where——

At this moment the footman, who was listening to their voluble remarks, lost his senses, how, he was never quite sure; but the last thing of which he was conscious was turning to stop the lady who was passing behind him. . . . Indeed, in the two or three minutes which followed his opening of the front door, one man plied him with questions, and the other two pervasively passed through the inner swing doors into the hall and began looking at the glass-cases. Then something that smelt uncommon strong seemed to go up his nose, and as he opened his mouth to shout, some one shoved a wad of cotton-wool between his lips and barred his speech, and the woman seemed to pinion his arms behind. . . .

The few servants left in the castle were having their midday meal at the time. Others had gone to a Saturday cricket match of Pulborough. . . .

Apparently whilst the footman lay half suffocated, unconscious, and pinioned, the robbers had swiftly and silently closed and locked two of the inner doors opening into the hall, and had passed into the museum—as it was called—which only communicated with the right side of the hall. They were thus, with the bolting of the front door, secured from intervention. They must have worked with swiftness, skill, the use of master-keys, and adroit knowledge.

About half-past two the housekeeper, surprised at the footman's delay in sending away the callers and returning to his unfinished meal, walked round to the hall to inquire and found the door locked. But everything within seemed silent. She turned back and looked through a side window, and thought she saw the tail end of a motor disappearing down the drive. She made a wide circuit to approach the hall, but found the door of access from the stairs and antechamber also locked on the other side. Now she was seriously alarmed and called out "Sidney!" She thought with her ear to the door she could hear strange gurgles in distant reply.

She then retraced her steps and ran out through some back door. Being Saturday afternoon, the gardeners were away playing cricket or looking on. The groom and chauffeur were absent from the stables for the same pur-

JEWELS AT DAVENSHAM CASTLE 99

pose, probably escorting their lady-loves. The coachman, now the principal motor-man, was up in London. . . . She distractedly returned along the drive and knocked loudly and repeatedly at the great front door.

Presently there were fumblings and shufflings, and a very sick footman in disordered plain clothes and unbuttoned collar gingerly unfastened the great door on the chain. Seeing the friendly, agitated woman's face through the slit, he drew to the door as if to shut it, detached the hook of the chain, and threw it open.

Then followed excited, unanswered questions on both sides, and a speedy examination of the glass-cases in the hall and the drawers and safe-doors of the museum. Two of the cases had been skilfully opened—evidently with skeleton keys—and most of their contents abstracted. The same had happened with at least a dozen drawers in the museum and one safe, as if the robbers had known more or less where to look. . . .

The housekeeper had to sit down on one of the sofas and think—think hard what she ought to do; while the footman went away to be sick, to wash, and to make himself tidy with a new collar and tie. It was by now 3 p. m. A train stopped at 4 p. m. at Davensham for Pulborough and London. The footman must drive her to the station, and she must go up and *see* the duke— better that than telegraphing. And, if there was time, she or Sidney could see the police at Davensham and give them an inkling of what had happened; get them to send out a sergeant to stay at the castle till she returned. . . .

Whilst she was absent *no one* except a member of the family was to be let in. . . .

Mrs. Townsend thus reached Victoria, after maddening checks and train changes, about six o'clock. The duke was away from home with the new king, attending to urgent State business; but the duchess was in, and, after a rapid interchange of news, agreed that Mrs. Townsend should hurry back to Victoria and catch the last train down, while her mistress would follow in a motor as soon as she had settled all urgent affairs.

The State business of the duke was so important that any thought of personal affairs had simply to be put aside for at least a week. The duchess at Davensham Castle seemed very calm about the losses, more upset as to dints and scratches. She hastened to get such damage and defacement as the thieves had inflicted scrupulously repaired, and reassured the servants with the visit of a very silent detective. . . .

The duke at last motored down. He examined, listened, nodded, pursed lips, inserted here and there an irrelevant query as to his wife's health, told Mrs. Townsend she had acted *admirably* and as he had always imagined she would have acted in such an emergency. He heard all that Sidney Graven could tell him (the narrative was now much embellished), and said in reply that all the steps which *could* be taken *had* been taken, and that the household might console itself in some slight degree for the disaster by realising that the jewels were insured.

But shortly afterwards authoritative announcements appeared in three newspapers to allay public anxiety. The

JEWELS AT DAVENSHAM CASTLE

duke's marvellous collection of jewels, it was stated, was safe and intact, and had a year or two ago all been transferred to London, where it had been recently sold advantageously to American museums and private collectors, as well as—in its more historical items—to the British Museum. The duke had felt that such a collection was beyond his means, and could not in his keeping be sufficiently safeguarded and at the same time be available for the study of qualified persons. He had therefore disposed of it in the manner stated, but had very generously implemented the bargain with the British Museum by several presents remarkable for their geological value.

But before disposing of this wonderful collection, which numbered among its contents the following remarkable stones—a variety of details were here given—he had had in the course of the last three years all its more interesting and beautiful details reproduced facsimile, as near as such things could be done, by very clever artificers. Practically only specialists and sharp-sighted connoisseurs could tell the imitations at a glance from the originals. These imitations were occasionally shown to interested visitors. . . . Unfortunately this hospitality had been grossly abused the other day by a party arriving in a motor who imagined they were looking at the original jewels. Much greater care would in future be taken in showing the collection of reproductions, which, though of no great intrinsic value, included remarkable examples of delicate work executed by Dutch, French, and English specialists in Hatton Garden.

The party of thieves who made away with the jewels never bothered, of course, about Southampton and an ocean steamer. They motored fifty miles to Newhaven by highways and—when passable—byways. They arrived there with an hour and a half to spare to get the motor safely lodged on the night mail-boat to Dieppe. They required to take the motor with them, as it was a vehicle specially arranged for their traffic, and had cunning nooks and hollows in the framework, and cushions devised for such purposes as the conveyance of jewels and lace. They made no fuss about the payment of legitimate charges, and were generous in tips. And the age was not sufficiently advanced for Customs' officers and mail-boat officials to be suspiciously inquisitive about motor construction. No passports were required in those blissful days. They gave an ample *pourboire* when the motor was landed at Dieppe, and left the quay on the road to Paris by 8. a. m.

Of course they were not going into or through Paris. They intended first to halt on some thoroughly empty, open down, with a good view all round, eat a hearty meal, and at last examine closely the booty they had carried off. Two hours' motoring at twenty-five miles an hour found them these surroundings. . . . They stopped, backed the car to the sward by the roadside, had *un bout de toilette,* and ate a hearty and much-needed breakfast—moreover, the ostentation of this meal at the French breakfast hour would distract the attention of any passer-by from the boxes in which the jewels were stored. . . .

Half an hour's examination of the booty—less on the part of the leader and his mistress—caused their chaps to fall. It was all an admirable, high-class fake, with

JEWELS AT DAVENSHAM CASTLE

the fakers' names minutely inscribed on the back. The Balas diamond was perhaps worth as paste £5; and the Gianpetri rubies might sell at £2 or £2, 10s. each. . . .

The lady of the party really gave way to a few tears, and she very seldom cried. "How *could* we have been such consummate idiots as to take everything for granted!" she exclaimed, getting up from sitting on the rug, and dusting the odds and ends of road-metal and grass off her travelling costume. The men whistled in low tones, and ground out muttered oaths of vague import. (But as a rule their language was no worse than in other well-clothed circles. For really shocking language, because of its genial utterance, you should mix with cheerful, shopkeeping costers on a Sunday morning in Marylebone.)

"Well!" exclaimed their leader, "we've been nicely done this time. They're nothing but a dam' clever lot of fakes!"

They decided to go on to Amsterdam and see Baarents for a final decision. After he had spent a silent half-hour passing their collection in careful review, he looked up at the leader of the party and said, "Two hundred pounds? I could sell zem for two hundred and fifty in the Rue de Rivoli as curiosities. Did you do them? Ve-ry clever!"

Their leader, more by motion than by words, withdrew from the transaction. They returned to the motor, put the jewels away with weary disdain, hid them better before they crossed the Belgian frontier; otherwise scarcely paused till they reached an hotel in Brussels.

Here they divided the jewels into four parcels, declared them non-dutiable in the Customs, and sent them registered, addressed to the Duke of Dulchester. Then after a few days' rest they went on to Ostend, where in the course of a summer season they won about £10,000 at the casinos, the races, and other places and occasions for gambling within the limits of the law.

NOT WHAT YOU MIGHT HAVE EXPECTED

IN the opening years of the nineteenth century, Armenians dwelling under Turkish rule or Turkish tyranny often bore surnames that were Greek in origin. I cannot tell you why. For instance, there was a well-known Armenian merchant at Liverpool in 1849 whose father had in some unrecorded way made a large fortune in Turkey under English patronage during the Napoleonic and the Russian Wars. His son, several years after the father's death, was seized with the fancy of coming to England and getting to know the English people. His Christian name was Aphthonios or Afton, but his surname was Bdellion, which I believe is in Greek the designation of an aromatic and—taken in a draught—stimulating herb, growing in Asia Minor. Perhaps the fortunes of the family had been founded in the eighteenth century by some enterprising Armenian druggist who had popularised the use of Bdellion Tea. However that may be, Mr. Bdellion, who had the unconscious bravery of landing at Liverpool in 1849, soon found that an additional vowel in his surname was all that was necessary to ensure a welcome among the hospitable Liverpudlians. So he wrote his name "Bedellion," and married an Englishwoman, the daughter of a North Country clergyman who had begun to study the affairs of the Armenian Church in his leisure time.

Whether or not he had been married before in Turkey to an Armenian cousin I should not like to aver. It really did not matter in those distant days, when Asia Minor was almost in another world. No one challenged his marriage in England, at any rate. He had come to speak English quite fluently by 1851, and had given much good advice about the exhibits of the Levant to the Commissioners of the Great Exhibition in Hyde Park.

Next followed the Crimean War. Bedellion returned to Constantinople at the beginning of the upset, and later proved a valuable intermediary between the British Generals and the Turks, since he spoke by that time with equal fluency, English, Turkish, Italian, and French. He was, in fact, so useful that when the War was over the question arose whether—since he had become a naturalised British subject—he should not be given a knighthood. But Queen Victoria had still a little prejudice to overcome about knighting persons who were not British subjects by birth. His son, however, afterwards Sir Anthony Bedellion, had the privilege of being born in England of an English mother; so, after he had in 1873 attained his majority, and presented the Liverpool hospital for Diseases of the Chest with £10,000, and in 1876 founded, in memory of his father just deceased, the Bedellion Ward in the St. Pancras Hospital, and erected a public drinking fountain in Mile End, it was decided to give him a baronetcy. These were the ostensible reasons cited by Lord Beaconsfield. The other motives were the strong support he gave to our diplomacy in the Near East, and his conversations with the Turkish Ministers which brought about the presentation of Cyprus.

NOT WHAT YOU MIGHT EXPECT

Sir Anthony, half English in blood, with all these advantages of wealth (he became a millionaire in 1880), expert knowledge of the Near East, could by that time aspire to marriage with the peerage; but he contented himself by proposing to the daughter of a well-connected baronet in 1880, when his age was twenty-eight. He led her to the altar of St. Peter's Church, Eaton Square, in which district he had acquired a magnificent town house. He was not at all an ill-looking man, unless he got into a temper. Then there was a hint of Asia Minor about his eyes and mouth, and his Armenian brachycephali seemed more evident. Otherwise, except that he had a very white complexion and luxuriant growth of black hair, beard, and moustache, he quite passed muster as an Englishman. His father was probably never seen in a temper outside his home. He was a good-natured man who attained his ends with little outburst of speech or action.

Sir Anthony married twice. By his first wife, daughter of Sir Cloudesley Shovell, he had four children: Afton, Anthony, Sara, and Eleanor. When she died in 1888, he waited two years, and then, in 1890, he married again; this time the daughter of an Irish peer. For five years they went about as Sir Anthony and the Hon. Lady Bedellion. Then, after the Conservatives came into power in 1895, Sir Anthony was raised to the peerage.

"Lord Baghdad, I suppose?" surmised an ill-natured ex-Minister. But no; Anthony resolved to have as British a title as possible. "Ashburnham" was pre-engaged; "Appledurham" was too quaint; "Aldworth" was a good selection, and the nearest village to the place they had taken in Berkshire. [They had gradually moved south from Liverpool, though they had a huge business in that city. But the value of it was now more than triplicated by their offices in London and Glasgow.]

The Hon. Eleanor Bedellion was born in 1886, and remembered no other mother than the lady of the second marriage, whom she came to know when she was four years old. Strangely enough, a vivid affection sprang up between them. Alice Combermere was an almost heart-broken bride in the first six months of her marriage. She was only twenty-one, and had hoped to marry—in time—one of the Shovells—a Captain Shovell, nephew of the first Lady Bedellion. He was extremely good-looking (she thought), but he was one of a large family, and poor. Her own brothers and sisters were many; the Viscount, her father, had lost much money of late—racing, Irish property, speculation. . . . The proposal from Sir Anthony had seemed to her mother almost a providential interposition. . . . There could be no question of anything but acceptance. Even to Alice the sacrifice seemed inevitable; and after all, her distant cousin and predecessor had not expressed herself as unhappy. She had died of one of those sequalæ of frequent confinements not mastered in those days by medical knowledge, and accepted as an expression of the Divine Will. Sir Anthony was Eastern in his passion for begetting children. . . . Alice herself, after four months of marriage, was enceinte. . . . Probably she too would die in childbirth. Meantime Eleanor was a dear, grave little thing and wanted her, and she clung to Eleanor; and through her, in the months which preceded the birth of her first child, she grew almost reconciled to her position.

The other stepchildren were far less nice. The elder boys, Afton and Anthony, had hard, Eastern eyes, loud voices; and though respectively only nine and seven and a half, seemed nearly as cognizant of the world as she was. Sara, the elder girl, though distinctly pretty—even one might say a beautiful child—was at six years old quite self-reliant and decidedly critical. Her eyes, like those of Eleanor's, were superb in their large size, their long lashes, and Eastern glamour of a dark iris; but whereas Eleanor's were lambent with a great love, Sara's were invincibly hard and measuring.

Of course, as this little story was being enacted in the 'nineties, in the case of a very rich family, everything was done decently and in order, and Alice, hampered with recurrent child-bearing, was not brought too frequently into contact with her stepchildren. Eleanor sought her company; she Eleanor's. Otherwise, they would not have become inseparable. The boys had a tutor, Sara had a governess, and a maid who might have been a nursemaid only that Sara, when no more than seven, called her "my maid" and ordered her about.

Alice did not die or even suffer very much in giving birth to her four children. Some exceedingly superior form of twilight sleep was brought about, even in those days, and she had a healthy constitution, strengthened by much rough-riding in the days when it was safe to ride about Ireland.

Her children were all more or less like their dominant father: they were alternately a boy, a girl, a boy, a girl.

Eight years covered these births from the date of her marriage; and at the end of this period Eleanor was twelve and Sara was fourteen. During the same period, Afton and Anthony grew larger and taller, and went through public schools—Afton, however, with an eye on Sandhurst, and an ultimate commission in the Guards; Anthony thinking more of money, and taking up a position in the great house of Bedellion & Sons, London and Liverpool.

Lord Aldworth in 1898 was forty-six or forty-seven. His eyes were a little bloodshot, his pale white face a little too fat. His head hair was cut quite short to make him look as English as possible; his thick moustache was severely clipped and brush-like, and otherwise, of course, he was clean shaven. Indeed he sighed with impatience at the thought of how much time had to be given up to being shaved by his accomplished valet twice a day. But that is one of the consequences of Armenian blood, counterbalanced, though it may be, by a diversity of talents.

He took, perhaps, less exercise than he should have done. Golf bored him to desperation—*such* a waste of time!—and fellow-golfers seemed to probe him for financial tips. He rode in the early morning in town, and in Berkshire, but did not spend more than an hour on horseback; and that was done less for the enjoyment of the morning world than as a gymnastic exercise to keep off the effects of too much food and too rich a dietary.

Alan Shovell, the nephew of the first Lady Bedellion, whom Alice had once hoped to marry, was far too poor and too good-looking to remain long a bachelor. A very rich American woman virtually proposed to him at a shooting party in Scotland, the autumn after Alice's marriage. And although he replied evasively at first, in the following winter he succumbed. She settled five thousand pounds a year on him, as pocket money, and they led a rather rackety life on her remaining income of an annual hundred thousand dollars. Sometimes she wished to be a great lady in England, and she would spend six months in a place she had taken on a high rental, trying to be "great." Then greatness to the full degree not coming quickly enough, she would have an attack of nerves or a *fausse couche,* and transfer herself to Venice or to Beni-Ounif in Algeria, and be excessively Venetian or Anti-Atlantean in a short space of time; while he, having got into Parliament, wanted to settle down, live seriously, and perhaps get into the Ministry.

Eleanor Bedellion meantime was growing up. She was fourteen in 1900: a tall, handsome girl, rather large made, musically endowed, inclined to be gravely beautiful when adult, with eyebrows rather too broadly marked over eyes that could be wells of love or pools of scorn. The straitest affection still bound her to her stepmother. Her sister Sara, by this time nearly seventeen was, with great difficulty kept within bounds of schooling and control. In Armenia she would by this age have been married and a mother—she had that constitution. Here she must still, if she observed the properties, listen to the instruction of governesses and tutors, wear dresses that did not reach her ankles—in days when grown-up dresses still swept the ground.

Lord Salisbury in 1898 sometimes referred to Lord

Aldworth as "My Armenian counterblast." Apparently he hoped his influence might prevail in diverting the Ministry, especially the Secretary of State for the Colonies, from too much concentration on South African affairs. Aldworth could hardly hear "South Africa" mentioned without giving way to intempestive denunciation of Rhodes. "The 'Rhodes' *we* ought to keep our minds fixed on," he would exclaim—so far as so secretive a man ever spoke out loud—"is the *Island* of Rhodes, the key-point of the Eastern problem."

His own purview of the "important" world, the Near East, the East, just took in Zanzibar on its south-western extremities, with Persia and Afghanistan on the northern angle of extension, Egypt somewhere about the middle, and the diverging lines of the scope of vision being farthest apart as they reached the Pacific Ocean. He was equally opposed to the extension of German ambition over Constantinople and Asia Minor. In short, he saw things as a glorified Armenian might have done. . . . If Germany was content with the Congo Basin and a great belt of Africa below, and even western Morocco, let her have them. As he grew older he became one idea-ed to a fatiguing extent. This embittered absorption in the affairs of the Levant, and especially in the future of the Turkish Empire, affected by degrees his health and his sanity of outlook, and brought about an envenomed quarrel with the Colonial Secretary, who was reported to have derided him.

Captain Alan Shovell was greatly stirred over the unfavourable turn things had taken soon after the South

NOT WHAT YOU MIGHT EXPECT 113

African War broke out, and further exasperated by his wife's behaviour in insisting on living all the year round at Beni-Ounif, where she was building herself a Moorish palace. Without long reflection he resigned his seat in Parliament and resumed army work in Cape Colony on Kitchener's staff at the beginning of 1900. His wife, expecting such a decision, gave herself in marriage to an Arab chief who had been educated at Marseilles, and invited Captain Alan to divorce her, which he was much too busy to do till Pretoria was taken. By this time he was a colonel and a D.S.O. He obtained a divorce in 1902, returned home with further military honours, and eventually met Alice, whom he had not seen for years.

She was by this time about thirty-three and a really beautiful woman. She felt herself occupying a detached position. Her husband was fifty years of age, and so much knit up in passionate wrangles about the East that he seemed almost to forget his wife's existence, except when affairs of State required her to make an appearance on his arm, or as a hostess at an evening party, a luncheon, or a dinner of effulgence. Eleanor was by now a girl of sixteen. Sara was engaged to be married to an Under-Secretary at the Colonial Office. Afton had just attained his majority and got his commission in the Guards; and Anthony was a student at Cambridge preparatory to working at the firm's head office.

Alice's own four children, two boys and two girls, varied in age from eleven to six. They all seemed too much like their father for her to feel impelled to do more than her duty by them.

We all know when we are sane that you cannot reason

with love; love—unhappily—will listen to no reason. When Alice met Colonel Alan Shovell in November, 1902, at a shooting-party, she felt all the old love return irresistibly, though she fought against surrender by shortening her visit and returning to town.

The boys were at school, except the youngest. Lord Aldworth was away at Liverpool, and very much upset at the trend of affairs in Turkey and Asia Minor. Eleanor was working hard at the town house in connection with a college she attended in Regent's Park, preparatory to Girton. She wanted to become a woman doctor. . . . "My dear," would say Alice, in these discussions, "you are going to be *much* too beautiful to do anything but marry, and you will be well dowered enough to be able to pick and choose a good husband." But Eleanor had thoughts and aspirations rising higher than domesticity.

However, when Alice met her in London in this month of November, she was ashamed to confide her own love trouble to the studious girl. She feared that Eleanor would shrink from her in horror if she did. . . . Then again, her youngest daughter Armida, suddenly showed herself seriously unwell—despite the bland assurances of the family doctor. It was some form of meningitis, and the child suddenly became unconscious and died in her mother's arms. This blow put all thought of Alan out of Alice's mind. . . .

Yet, in the spring, she began to recur to him in her thoughts. He came to the house increasingly, and she could not summon up words to repel him. Eleanor, however, seemed to guess her mother's trouble, the underlying cause of this renewal of her beauty, the return—one might say—of a look of youth in her eyes and the outline of her face. She became constant in her attendance on Alice, even putting on one side her engrossing studies to take a third place in the meetings and excursions. Sometimes she received him instead of Alice. . . .

Oddly enough, this made her stepmother jealous and pettish, though she would not have confessed it. . . . She did not like to take an overt step to secure an unobstructed interview with Alan. She still felt afraid of giving way, of disgracing herself, losing the care of her children, the privileges of her high position, becoming a divorced woman (the thought of it made her shudder). Perhaps, most of all, she shrank from the loss of Eleanor's society. . . .

Then there were times of torture in which she asked herself whether, after all it might not be Eleanor and Eleanor's dowry which were the real attraction in Alan's visits; and whether Eleanor might not herself have fallen in love with Alan? . . .

One day, in the late spring of 1903, she felt distraught. She was seized with an intense desire to see Alan—not here, not in her husband's house, but at his own flat, overlooking the embankment—to tell him everything—to ask him not to come and see them any more—to implore his pity—advice—— She dressed hurriedly, yet carefully, inconspicuously. . . . She would walk away from the great house to a side street, with her veil down—a hansom—and drive to his flat. . . .

As she opened the hall door there were two men on the

step about to ring. . . . One was a policeman, the other a messenger from the House of Lords.

"Lady Aldworth——?"

"Yes: what is it?"

"We—er—we come to bring you rather bad news. . . . Er . . . Lord Aldworth——"

"What is it? Speak quickly. . . ."

"Lord Aldworth has had a fit—in the Peers' Gallery—House of Commons. . . . They are bringing him home. . . . We wished to prepare your Ladyship. . . ."

So it was; only that when Lord Aldworth reached his door he was dead.

A speech contravening his statements and obstructing his futile plans for Britannicising the Levant had been delivered that afternoon in the House of Commons. He had—improperly, of course—risen to utter some inarticulate protest, and had collapsed with some effusion of blood on the brain. . . .

Eleanor, who had just gathered that her stepmother was going out on foot and had prepared herself to forestall her—if possible—at Colonel Shovell's address, came into the hall at this moment and helped Lady Aldworth to bear the blow. . . .

Lord Aldworth's will left Afton grumbling and sulky; otherwise it gave general satisfaction. Afton received a lump sum of £250,000, and a further share in the firm's profits, so long as he did not remove from its capital more than £100,000. Each other child and the testator's widow were willed, severally, £100,000, not, however, to be removed from investment in Bedellion & Sons' concerns. These bequests still left a million sterling of the estate to be accounted for. Out of this, death duties on all the bequests were to be paid; and the remaining balance was left as part of the firm's capital, when £50,000 had been spent on small legacies to servants and employees, and to charities and endowments connected with Armenia.

A year afterwards, Lady Aldworth married Sir Alan Shovell, K.C.B., M.P. They led ever afterwards, down to the time of writing, lives of the most perfect happiness. Eleanor stayed with them much, at first, but of course, less as the years went by, and she obtained her medical degree, and started a practice of growing importance as a woman's doctor in Harley Street. She refused innumerable offers of marriage, excited by her beauty and her wealth.

"GOOD-NIGHT, OLD MAN!"

THE scene of this story was a bedroom in a very nice nursing home in Beaumont Street, west of Portland Place; the characters visible are only three: Major Henry Oldham, Major Maurice Mansfield, and Miss Grace Goodenough.

Major Henry Oldham has been a young country squire, just about to settle down after ten years' roaming at large, when the War broke out and soon involved him in it. Perhaps he had been a soldier before; perhaps he was—son of a wealthy cotton spinner—so essentially a soldier of the officer class that he was given a commission six weeks after the War broke out. Anyhow, he has served stolidly and unemotionally all through the four years and three months of war, and left it a Major.

Maurice Mansfield, before he was badly wounded and insufficiently gassed—had he breathed in a little more he would have ceased to suffer—had been an athletic University man with about four hundred a year of his own, who had passed for the Bar when the War broke out, but had had no time to create a practice. Maurice, also, had fought all through the War, first in France, then at Salonika, then in East Africa, and lastly again in France, where in the dogged struggle of 1918 he had been wounded here-there-and-elsewhere and finally gassed. Some sort of a recovery had been patched up

"GOOD-NIGHT, OLD MAN!" 119

at a field hospital in France, so that he was invalided back to London after the War ended in the Armistice. His wounds were chiefly surface ones in face and neck, which had scarred his features, and in his despondent outlook materially robbed him of his good looks. His gassing had been much more serious. It had led to various internal complications, and soon after he reached England from the field hospital he was obliged to enter a nursing home and submit to an operation from which, at the opening of this story, he was making a much better recovery than he would allow himself to believe.

One effect of imperfect gassing in those days—the fully perfected form finished you off, once and for all—was to induce considerable melancholy of disposition, even in the young and naturally hopeful. At Christmas-time, 1918, and in a really nice nursing home, such as this one was, Maurice's prospects seemed to Maurice nearly hopeless. How was he *ever* going to make a career and money at the Bar? Why had he ever been dam' fool enough to go in for such a career? Preparation for it had covered five years of University education and law study for the passing of examinations; and then, when he had been called to the Bar in 1913, nothing very much had happened; he was still awaiting briefs when War broke out in August, 1914, and he had hastily sought an officer's commission.

He had marvellous escapes during the first three years of the War; intense fatigues; devilish bad luck in saving situation after situation—at Calais in 1915, at the Vardar crossings in 1916, on the Ruvuma River in 1917, and at Amiens in 1918—and getting little reward or promotion.

At the end of the War he was still only a Major and a M.C.

And a month before the War ended there had come on him the crowning mishap of intercepting in face and neck a shower of stones sent up by a bursting shell; and, as he lay prostrate and insensible, inhaling the expiring effort of a gas wave, which penetrated the torn gas mask he was wearing.

He was picked up and taken to the hospital at Bapaume. Here, when he dimly regained consciousness, or a consciousness that extended beyond the pain of the face wounds, the struggle against suffocation, streaming eyes, phlegm-encumbered throat and nose, he found himself in the charge of two alternating nurses, or a nurse and a matron. The latter, after about ten days, he realised was a beautiful woman. She was known as "Sister Grace." A month later he ascertained her name in the world-beyond to be Grace Goodenough. . . .

The nearly unbearable pains of his face wounds awaking from numbness through the extraction of the gravel fragments; the appalling catarrh of the mustard gas: were sufficient conjointly to keep his thoughts for the first seven or eight days wholly occupied with the problem of struggling back to life. But when three or four more days had gone by, when his eyes could be uncovered, a little space grew and expanded in his consciousness for other human beings besides himself. One day he heard it said by some one in the next bed that, the night before, poor Jevons—Captain Jevons—had "gone West;" and he moved his black and swollen lips to say, "Poor devil!" Then a little later he began to remark—with an audible

"GOOD-NIGHT, OLD MAN!"

groan—what a beautiful face in nurses's uniform bent over him, ever and again removed and renewed his plasters, exorcised somehow his choking phlegm, gave him food or drink or medicine.

As often these services were rendered by the hands of Sister Juliet. She too was attractive, but a little "brisk." He learnt afterwards she was the daughter of an Oxford don. She had a charming voice and kind eyes, but her figure was somewhat too short and plump for romance, and she seemed emphatically of the second rank by the side of her fellow-worker, Sister Grace.

When bed-to-bed confidences were possible—there were five other fellow-sufferers in the ward besides himself—he gathered that this was the accepted opinion: that Sister Grace was a goddess, and Sister Juliet a dam' good sort. Three of the wounded officers were already married men; one knew himself—poor wretch—to be unmarriageable. Jevons was dead, and Mansfield with a thrill realised that *he* was an unencumbered bachelor. But to all alike it seemed as though union in matrimony with Sister Grace would be worth having suffered all they had suffered in the War.

If you could visualise Grace as she was then, this ratio would seem feeble. But if, reader, you have ever been gassed and are recovering, are beginning dimly to realise hope beyond the limits of despair, the indication of dawn relieving night, you would still rate your past mountain of misery as a very lofty alp; and your consenting to adopt a normal life of marriage, love, and income-winning as a gracious act on your part, requiring beauty and fortune as its reward.

For rumour, based on the discreet admissions of Sister Juliet, endowed her colleague with a substantial income of her own. Grace Goodenough had actually eight hundred a year left her by her father, a celebrated, knighted surgeon in Harley Street, who had lost his life from blood-poisoning in the second year of the War. Juliet Harborn, wishing to do her colleague justice, probably doubled the estimated income left to Grace, and the wounded officers regarded Grace consequently with increased awe, as even more beyond their reach than if she had been a poorer woman.

Well: fighting finished about November 11th with the signing of the Armistice, and by the end of that month Maurice was well anough to be moved to London for further examination; for, alas, there were complications through the gas poisoning and the need for a surgeon's operation and treatment in a nursing home. Grace recommended him to enter one she knew in Beaumont Street, intimately connected with her father's practice, and promised him if he followed her advice to come and see him there as soon as she could return to England.

So here we are back at the beginning of my story. Maurice has had one rather serious operation, and a week later a second, a minor one; and is now considered by the surgeon as fit to receive an occasional visitor. His father is dead, his brother and his sisters are married and scattered, and do not interest him. His mother is a dear old thing, but of rather inadequate mind and limited outlook. She has been the wife of a country squire in Warwickshire. Her husband once had five or six thousand a year, which was quite enough in his lifetime to keep up the family estate. But half his money has passed to his children, and on the other half his widow finds it difficult to live in the big, gaunt house without shutting up the moiety and turning herself into a farmer. She has paid one visit to her son and then has returned to her poultry farming and her milch cows.

Maurice's few friends have been killed or wounded, or driven by circumstances to the uttermost ends of the earth. The only army acquaintance who seems to care anything about him is Major Oldham, whom he has met here and there in the course of the past four years. Oldham came to see him at Bapaume, and in spite of stolidity was greatly struck with the charm and talent of Sister Grace. As, however, he was not wounded and only a visitor, Sister Grace did not reciprocate by taking any interest in him. But when Maurice had got over the worst of his last operations in London, Oldham called to see him, and for the last ten days has looked in every day at the visiting hours.

This is kind, Maurice feels; in fact he argues to himself that Oldham must have a tender heart behind his stolidity and his flaxen moustache.

The two women who run this nursing home are Miss Lightwell (elderly, immensely clever) and Miss Ransome. I could write a good deal about Miss Ransome, but it would not belong to this story. She was said to be the daughter of an Admiral, about thirty-five, an angel imprisoned in a human form; deft, cultivated, tender, witty. I doubt whether they could have made the Home pay; and I expect by now Miss Ransome must have gone back to heaven, and Miss Lightwell have been appointed

Superior in an Anglican Sisters' Convent. But I tend to be discursive, and must reluctantly keep these women out of my story, especially, as Grace Goodenough is returning to it.

Grace's father, who had died from the scratch of a scalpel in 1915, had made much use of the Home founded by Margaret Lightwell of Oxford, and Judith Ransome ostensibly from Cambridge. Grace in her nurse's training had run in and out. She may even afterwards, when she had a little money to invest, have put it in the Home. At any rate, she advised Maurice, and many a previous patient in whom she was interested, to place themselves finally in the hands of Misses Lightwell and Ransome to get cured of wounds and their consequence, or at the worst to be tenderly nursed to the closing of eyes and the passing away.

Soon after Maurice had had his "bad" operation, and while they were waiting for him to recover tone to undergo the supplementary one, Grace had returned from France and presented herself at the Home; which was no doubt the reason why Henry Oldham's visits to his damaged comrade became as assiduous as the restrictions of the Home permitted—an hour a day in the afternoon.

Maurice, in his isolation, felt these daily calls to be very kindly meant, but they became boring eventually; and besides, the weary presence of a stout, well-fed, well-dressed, rather silent individual irked his irritable nerves. Oldfield also inspired jealousy. He had gone through the War nearly as much as Maurice, but he had come out of it unwounded. He hadn't even had dysentery or malaria fever. A sprain here, a strain there, a

"GOOD-NIGHT, OLD MAN!" 125

bad influenza cold in one place (which he described as a gas attack), an injured toe-nail in another. Those were all the ills he could recount. His attentions were well meant; but what did they mean?

Like a flash the solution occurred to him in a sleepless night. Oldfield was in love with Grace Goodenough! This obvious fact suddenly paralysed his thoughts. Report gave his friend—how the word *"friend"* is cheapened!—his "friend" twenty thousand a year. He himself had four hundred, outside his army pay, which in time would be commuted to a small pension. . . . He had a smashed face and a broken career. . . . Competition was hopeless. . . .

In the climax of these glomy thoughts about 3 a. m., his eyes turned to the little bedside table, between his pillows and the wall. Yes. It stood there still, his last resort against unendurable agony and hopelessness—a small bottle of veronal tabloids, ingeniously mislabelled "Quillett's Cough Drops."

He had secured this bottle at the very opening of the War—at any rate, he had it with him in Salonika. The deadliness of the drug was not then fully appreciated. . . . Maurice in Salonika had washed off the label and substituted another removed from some bottle sold at a Levantine store: "Quillett's Cough Drops."

Wherever he went henceforth he had carried Quillett's Cough Drops with him, sometimes concealed in his haversack, sometimes placed discreetly within reach at his bedside. He had told his soldier servant to look carefully after it, and never to venture to taste one himself. . . . There they were still, peeping out with a little cotton-wool stopping on top, from behind a tiny clock, a pen-and-ink stand, and a minute writing-case. Six of the globules or tabloids dissolved in water or scrunched up and washed down ought to do the trick—carry him off quietly, peacefully into oblivion. . . .

He dropped off into slumber, however, at this stage, exhausted by the violence of his thoughts. All through the next morning he was restless and fretful, and his temperature was again one degree above normal.

Grace Goodenough was absent all that day, though once he thought he heard her voice talking to Sir Peter. . . . At tea-time Maurice expressed a wish to see Major Oldfield if he called. Oldfield did call, was shown in, and accepted a cup of tea and a slice of cake. . . .

"Oldfield, old chap. I—I want to ask you an indiscreet question. . . . Yet I'm sure you won't mind. . . . We've been in some tight places together. . . . What are you feeling—I mean, have you any idea—Grace Goodenough, you know. . . . *Are* you and she engaged?"

These questions caused him such mental agony that they must have sent up his temperature one more degree. . . .

Henry Oldfield is rather taken aback. But he has intended this afternoon or evening to propose, to jolly well fix the matter up, to wait in the guests' parlour till Grace does come in and just put the question to which she is pretty certain to give assent. Indeed, he is so sure of the answer to the offer of his twenty thousand a year, that he thinks it wise to put old Maurice out of doubt at once. A chap with a smashed face and a constitution ruined by gas could not for a moment suppose——

"GOOD-NIGHT, OLD MAN!" 127

"Well, old man, since you put the question so plainly, I may as well say Grace and I are engaged. I'm waiting on here this evening to see her home. Just for a day or two, till I give you the tip, we don't want it talked about. No congrats at present. Tell you *when*. . . . Of course I've been sweet on her, ever since the old fighting days, when I first saw her at Bapaume. But I thought I'd wait to see how she panned out in home surroundings. *Now*, I simply can't do without her. . . . What's the matter? Want the window shut? It's only open at the top—and it's quite mild. . . ."

"No. Never mind the window—or anything else. . . . I've got a bit tired; that's all. . . . *Good-night, old man! Don't bother any more. . . . Good-night. . . .*"

Henry goes out, a little puzzled. "He's gettin' a bit fretful, poor old fellow. However, I'll wait in the parlour and ask 'em to let Grace know I'm waitin' for her there," are his framed thoughts (I can suppose) as he leaves Maurice's room.

Maurice, left alone, groans several times in self-pity, and then resolves to be through with it while the China tea gives him courage and resolution. He reaches out for Quillett's Cough Drops, knocks out six, which he was always told was a fatal dose, and drops them into his cool half-cup of tea. This he puts on one side, to give the drug time to dissolve. . . . An attendant comes in to take away the tray. He indicates by gesture that he has reserved the cup for a further purpose. She leaves him after a little tidying up.

Half an hour later he awakes from a tiny doze,

stretches out his hand for the teacup, finds the tabloids dissolved, shuts his eyes and resolutely drinks down the tea, which tastes in a sickly way of lemon.

Three or four hours afterwards, his eyes open from a peaceful slumber, and before he can speculate on whether he is gazing on heaven or hell, he descries Grace standing by the bedside and looking down on him. This is somehow so delightful, whether he be dead or alive, that he shuts his eyelids and dozes for two minutes before reopening them. She is still looking down on him. He groans.

"Oh, *don't* make that ugly noise, dear Major Mansfield, unless it is you *really* feel bad. You look *so* much better, and as to me, I am full of joy. I've been staying here an hour watching you sleep. I waited for you to wake to tell you I have seen Sir Peter this afternoon, and he says the last diagnosis is *most* satisfactory. You are not only going to *live,* but you're going—emphatically—to *recover* —to be *well* and *strong* again. You'll be convalescent in a month, and all my trouble and anxiety won't have been in vain. . . ."

She pauses lest her voice should break. Her eyes in the dim lamp-light are like jewels with unshed tears. . . .

"I don't *want* to live," groans Maurice, turning his head away so that he may not see her.

Grace is about to utter a protest; then checks herself.

"I dare say you don't at this moment. . . . The weather outside is wretched—another fog has come on— the war problems are complex: but—but—*I* want you to live—to be cured—to be strong again. . . ."

"GOOD-NIGHT, OLD MAN!"

There is something in her tone that speaks more strongly than any words. . . .

"*You?*" He turns gingerly on account of the scarcely healed surgeon's wound. . . . "*You?* But you are going to be married? . . ."

"I hope I am—some day——" she answers, looking down at the bedclothes and giving them a deft pull here and there to straighten things. . . .

" . . . to that beast of an Aldham. . . . Though I am damned ungrateful, seeing how often he has called here to cheer me up—*cheer* me up!" (with bitterness).

"What *nonsense,* what *wicked* nonsense!" she answers with quick anger, and speaking not as a nurse but as an indignant woman. "Who can have put such an idea into your head?"

"*He* did. Told me so—what was it? Three or four hours ago. . . . That's why I took the veronal. . . ."

"Veronal?" she questions, her eyes roving round the lodgments of the bed.

His right hand dumbly indicates the little bottle behind the writing-case. Her brow clears and she gives a silvery little laugh. . . .

"*Poor* darling! Do you suppose we *trusted* you, delirious or in pain, with *veronal* close at hand, even though you had named it Quillett's Cough Drops? If that is the same bottle you had at Bapaume, we spotted the veronal in it and confiscated the tabloids, replacing them by harmless digestive or laxative sugar-plums. . . ."

"Then nothing's going to happen to me?"

"Nothing bad, that I can think of; but if you have swallowed six or eight, it may equal in effect one liver pill.

Of course, I don't approve *in the least* of patients prescribing and taking their own medicines. But we thought in the uncertain days it would fret you to be cut off the apparent means of immolation, so we substituted a harmless cathartic for a deadly drug.... But I am wasting time, I want to make it *quite* clear there's *not one particle of truth* in your ridiculous fancy about—about—Major Oldfield. I hardly ever speak to the man, and he has never made me such an offer. And if he *had,* I"—tossing her head—"I should have told him I had already lost my heart—to —to—you——"

Maurice: "Darling! . . . *Darling! . . ."*

(Silence.)

She has bent over the prostrate figure to kiss gently the poor, scarred face.

FREDERICK'S REMORSE

IF I had known him then—instead of only knowing *of* him—I should have defined Frederick Hathergill in early times as "rather a boor, on the borders of gentility." In 1912 he must have been about twenty-three, the younger son of a fox-hunting squire—if they still hunted foxes in Herefordshire—who let and mismanaged about three thousand acres in the western part of that county. His mother had died when he was a little boy, and he had grown up rather uncared for under the hazy supervision of aunts on both sides. The aunts generally got married, even if a little elderly, before they had supervised very long the household of Squire Hathergill, for Herefordshire, like Suffolk, is a great marrying county.

Squire Hathergill, indeed, looked back with surprise when he reached the age of sixty, and wondered why it was *he* had not married again after his darling Rose had died. He had loved her as much as he loved anything that was not a horse or a hound or a fox; his finances, to be sure, might have been quoted as a reason, unless he could pick up a good dowry; but their condition would not have deterred him. He was a widower at the age of forty-five or forty-six; but his mind was so occupied with disastrous agriculture, failure of hops, failure of parsnips —or whatever else it is you ought to grow in lovely Herefordshire fields—with fox-hunting in the winter and early spring, cub-hunting in October and November, attendance at races between May and July, and cattle shows, haymaking, hop-picking, partridge-shooting, pheasant-shooting at other times in the year—it was only when he had reached the age of sixty, and began to look back, that he realized he might have married again.

Frederick, meantime, had grown up a very good-looking fellow, versed in most country sports, rather cruel to animals, and unsparing in his courtships of country girls. The girls took the matter lightly and always married somebody else, later on, of their own station. Frederick had three elder brothers. One had taken up the Army as a career, and was lost to sight in India; the second had become a naval lieutenant, and cared only for gunnery; the third had just been called as a barrister, and was trying to maintain himself in London on an allowance from his father, and short stories for weekly papers.

His eldest sister had something wrong with her back, which required a great deal of lying down, as her father would never go to the expense of having her properly examined and cured. She kept house for her father in an incomplete fashion. The second sister was married; and the third, the youngest member of the family, was just passing at the age of eighteen from the bouncing schoolgirl to the staider, slimmer maiden who expects to come out at the third Court of the next season under the tutelage of a second cousin.

Frederick had had a very chequered career at Rugby, and narrowly missed once or twice being expelled for discreditable reasons. He showed no aptitude for college,

FREDERICK'S REMORSE 133

so there was little question of a university career. After some hesitation, his parent—who by some twist of disposition liked him better than his staider brothers—made him pupil to his estate agent, in the hope that he might be educated in time to manage the parental property.

Amethyst Willscombe was the daughter of the Vicar of Bromley St. Margaret, the nearest village and the parish of Squire Hathergill's estate two miles away. She was called Amy for short, her fantastic "jewel" name having been bestowed by her mother, who died when she was a little girl. Amy Willscombe must have been about twenty-two in the spring of 1914. She was her father's only daughter, and for two years had kept house for him, enabling him thus to save a little money previously spent on the salary of a professional housekeeper. Her two brothers were older than herself, and first one, then the other, had gone out as an engineer and a chemist to a South African mining enterprise.

Amy was a good girl, pretty, outside the limits of a professional beauty, moderately clever, rather well educated, somewhat ambitious, and a little restless at having to sink her aspirations after a career in keeping house at the Rectory, with the slender chance of marrying any one who could have the outlook of a gentleman and was indifferent to a dowry.

She lived in an inaccessible part of Herefordshire. It was all very well to boast that the people in a village seven miles away spoke Welsh with avidity. Bromley St. Catherine was a long railway journey from civilisation. Her former school friends would come down for a fortnight's stay in June, July, or August, and expatiate on the heavenly peace, the perfect quiet, the masses of wild flowers, the abundance of cream, and the quantities of eggs and honey in this sylvan retreat five miles—the Hathergills were only three—from a railway station in direct communication with London. *They* did not have to live here through all the other months of the year.

Amy had started a rock-garden the year before, and tried to satisfy her ambition to some extent by trifling with botany and trading through the *Exchange and Mart* in saxifrages, aubretias, and ramondias. She developed the miserable lean-to fowl-house into a miniature poultry farm in a disused meadowlet; she obtained a nanny-goat as the nucleus of a herd of cheese producers. She tried in various other ways to put into operation novel ideas of employment for women learnt at her school in Bath.

These activities and a general roving quest for pretty women to look at attracted the attention of Frederick Hathergill. He had, of course, known Amy cursorily from his childhood, but had never thought her worth much notice till she returned home from a finishing school and became a distinctly good-looking young woman. His eldest sister Grace had taken a liking to her, wistfully enough; thought her very modern; wished she could do something to refine and modulate her own much younger sister, Betty. By the beginning of 1914, Amy had got into the habit, whenever the red clay lanes were not too muddy, of bicycling over to Hathergill Grange for morning consultations or for afternoon tea. In her innermost heart she confessed to a strong liking for Frederick, though she heard bad tales of him from the village peo-

FREDERICK'S REMORSE

ple. She decided to be on her guard—to continue to call him "Frederick," as they had grown up together, but not "Fred," and under no circumstances whatever, "Freddums," after Betty's style.

Frederick could hardly ever be induced after he was sixteen to come to church, but in less orthodox ways he became increasingly a visitor to Bromley. He helped Amy with her rock-garden, both in hunting for rare plants in the hills, and in overcoming the sheer difficulties of strenuous excavation of stones and lugging them to the long bank on which the rockery was established. He performed many feats of strength which Amy secretly admired. Gradually, without any offer made or accepted, without any reference to the two fathers, they drifted into a sort of engagement. Amy permitted—with remonstrances—an occasional kiss; she longed to return it, but instinctively dreaded the outburst of sexual frolic, of rough play it might occasion. And then, what means had Frederick to marry on? None worth speaking of. He knew a lot about the Turf, much about guns and game-preserving, but only as a pupil of his father, who allowed him a hundred and fifty pounds a year. . . .

Then came the declaration of War. Western Herefordshire only realised the dramatic change in affairs on the 5th of August, 1914. Frederick came over to Bromley Rectory with a new humility to consult the Rector and attempt to hug Amy behind the doors. The Rector was abstracted from his prehistoric studies—this part of Herefordshire was particularly prehistoric—carried down through Gibbon to Hodgkin, and from Alison to the

Crimea and the newspapers of to-day, and induced to give an opinion on the development of Mediterranean affairs. For even then rusticities felt that, though the conflict had broken out between France and Germany, it was only a preliminary to the struggle in the Balkans and Asia Minor.

Soon after this, Frederick went to Hereford and enlisted, his father cordially approving. Frederick's barrister brother did the same, and so the four sons of the elderly gentleman were all caught into the War; and Frederick disappeared from Amy's observation for some three months.

Then in November 1914 she heard he was back at the Grange with a sub-lieutenant's commission in a cavalry regiment. And one Saturday morning he came over "to see the Rector and to say good-bye." He brought a change of evening clothes in a new suit-case, and seemed to Amy greatly smartened up, dangerously good looking. His hands, for instance, which months ago were more often those of a farm labourer than of a gentleman, were now well kept, hardened, rutted inside, tanned on the outside, but with clean and well-cut nails. His moustache was smartly clipped, his hair smooth and shortly cut.

His manners were distinctly improved, or rather they had come into existence. He opened doors for a lady, spoke civilly and respectfully to her father, and listened quite a reasonable time to his long stories of what Herefordshire was like in the Druids' days and under Roman rule.

On the following Sunday morning he actually volunteered to attend the morning service with Amy, and though he slept through her father's sermon, he woke up

FREDERICK'S REMORSE

at the end with a charming smile of apology, and escorted her back, lover-like, to the Rectory. He hung about while she arranged the flowers on the luncheon table, and set forth the dessert of oranges, medlars, and walnuts.

Their afternoon together was delicious—dreamlike, Amy thought—though now and then she felt obliged to restrain his encircling arm or avoid his too passionate kisses. But she felt very much in love herself, though she set up this thin armour of restraint. After lunch was over and her father had retired for his nap, they went a long, vague walk, which ended on the dried heather of a hillside. Here they sat almost in a dream, he with his arm round her waist, unrebuked, and she every now and then letting her head rest on his shoulder. . . .

Then home to tea. Firelight only, at first, in her father's study, her father beginning to show a real interest in the War. He halted a little at Crimean times, but by Amy and Frederick he was gently led down to the present day, through the Franco-German struggle of 1870, the Russian attempt to get Constantinople in 1878, the struggle for the Sudan, and the Boer War at the end of Queen Victoria's reign.

Amy was proud of the little dinner she had put together, and her father had insisted on groping in his cellar for some real old Port to give Frederick a parting toast. Frederick would have to take an early breakfast the next morning and then be fetched by a groom and trap to say good-bye at the Grange and catch a morning train to London. He was to start for France two days later. . . .

She said good-night to him, therefore, at ten. Her father liked going to bed early. As she brushed her hair and plaited it for the night, she could hear their "goodnights" and the shutting of their doors. How Frederick was improved! There now seemed some prospect of marriage in a year or two if he got promoted. . . . If he was killed? No! Shuddering, she said to herself she must not *think* that. So at last she lit a night-light and placed it in a thick glass tumbler on the little bedside table, and got into bed. She was just beginning to pass into sleep when she heard a slight creak, and her bedroom door was quietly opening. "Frederick!" she exclaimed in a low voice, "is that you?"

"Yes. Don't call out. . . . I will explain. . . ." He turned and locked the door. She saw by her night-light he was in pyjamas. Something seemed to choke her— the beating of her heart, perhaps. She tried to expostulate, but felt it was a weary sham. She was in his arms, and, after all, they were going to be married at his next long leave. . . .

She slept little that night. Happiness too intense, dread lest her soldier lover should be surprised by the household kept her awake. At five o'clock she roused him and made him return to his own bedroom. Then she dressed herself and went downstairs before the cook, to prepare an early breakfast. At eight o'clock—feeling in reality very much ashamed of himself—he left in the dogcart, and she felt all she loved and cared for went with him.

He had so moved her that the idea of living on at home on the borders of Wales, doing nothing except idiotic gardening and housekeeping, seemed intolerable. She roused aunts in London. She persuaded one that was

FREDERICK'S REMORSE

widowed and rather damaged to take her place here with her father "until the War should be over." She arranged with another to board her, to give her a passing refuge and some motherly assistance while she studied to play the part of an efficient nurse. For two months after Frederick's departure she watched her own condition carefully. But at the end of three months, finding she was not going to become "an unmarried mother," she shut all these thoughts out of her mind and studied with quiet determination to become an efficient Red Cross nurse.

And Frederick?

Frederick wrote at long intervals two jejune letters from France, with various misspellings of French names. They were not specially lover-like, but then letters of this kind were liable to be read by any one. He made no allusion to any of the cautious sentences in her letters. Could they have reached him?

At the end of a year's training she was sent as a Red Cross nurse to the outskirts of the War area in France. This was in December 1915. She was mildly excited at the thought that she might see Frederick. Where he was, she did not know, but she wrote to the prescribed address to let him understand that she had come to France and might, first of all, he heard of at Amiens.

No answer came to this particular letter, and she herself, as the months of 1916 passed by, became so caught up in the hospital work, so absorbed in the vivid dangers of her life from bombs, gas attacks, aircraft bombardment, that Frederick's silence was at worst a mild source of sorrow as suggesting his death. Poor boy! . . .

When she thought of that night of love, in November

1914, she—so to speak—shook her head at her untrained, impulsive self. How distant that time seemed! She could never now have yielded herself as she had done then. Perhaps, all things considered, it was forgivable, understandable. It could be explained in a medical work, with initials for surnames, as an unpremeditated surrender to sexual attraction. It must become in her mind a closed incident, to be atoned for (only, why should *women* always have to make atonement, and not men?)—wiped out by a life of continuous devotion in her present sphere. On the other hand, if Frederick should live through the War and they should come together again, very likely they would marry and only refer to the night of 8th November shamefacedly with "Hush! Let us forget it, dear!"

In a purely motherly way she felt in love with all fighting men—British, Belgian, and French—and even not what you could call cruel towards the Germans, except the Kaiser and the leading generals. The sight of one terrible wound after another, of shattered limbs and protruding entrails, had quenched entirely, had put cleanly out of her mind, any paltry interest in sex. She was prepared to correct concupiscence with a dose, and prescribe for the regularisation of love with no more emotion than would be caused by attending to looseness of the bowels.

Nevertheless, she read with considerable emotion in in May 1917 of an exceedingly gallant and successful episode in the career of "Major" ("So he has become a major!" she commented) "Frederick Hathergill," a dismounted cavalry officer, who had, with a party of his men carried a German position near Loos, thereby saving our

FREDERICK'S REMORSE

front from perpetual harassing attacks. The whole thing was theoretically wrong, but under Hathergill's leadership it had worked out practically right: the Germans had been taken completely by surprise. Major Hathergill had been wounded in the leg, but when his action was followed up by a strong force from our lines, he gave over to them the captured position and retired to have his wounds treated.

Well! She felt herself worthy—after all *she* had done and passed through, and the decoration *she* already wore—of being a Colonel's bride—if that was the promotion Frederick had gained. So she wrote him a cordial letter to the home address, telling him of her career, adventures, mishaps, and successes, and of the position she had conquered under the Red Cross. She made it clear that she had written to him twice before in answer to his own two letters, and although she wrote a discreet letter that any one might read—his father being notoriously reckless about opening and reading all his children's correspondence—she let it be seen that her feelings toward him were the same.

A month went by before there was any answer. When it came, though she recognised the handwriting (while noting its changes), she was concerned as head-nurse in a very important, critical operation on another young colonel. She was so anxious for its success—he was one of the Australians, and a fine specimen of humanity—that two days passed before she suddenly recollected there was an unopened letter from Frederick put away in her dispatch-box. She read it through twice, not quite grasping its meaning, or else it was that she still felt so anxious over her Australian patient that she could not give clear attention to what Frederick had scrawled. Yet this was it. He said very little about his leap to publicity and fame, but was telling her of having met here (in Yorkshire), where he was convalescing, an heiress with lots of money, whom he was going to marry as soon as his leg was healed. The story was told so jerkily, and with such attempts to be funny and jovial, that to a puzzled, anxious person it was not at first comprehensible.

Yet when Amy came to understand the full purport of the letter, it somehow took the colour out of life. She again remembered vividly, with details she thought she had forgotten, his wooing of her in the November night. *How* could men forget so easily when women remembered indelibly?

She looked at herself in the glass of her little room, with its narrow, tidy bed and the telephone by the bedside table. She was twenty-two in the summer of 1914, and her twenty-fifth birthday was near at hand. Did she look her age? Her follow-nurses, when they had leisure to think of such things, assured her she was "beautiful;" but a Frenchwoman had added *magistrale* as a qualifying phrase. She had attained exceptional promotion by this "magistral" quality, by cultivating a certain sternness which purposely repelled any approach of flirtation.

Heigh-ho! She did not answer Frederick's letter, and she went on attending Colonel Apperley, the Australian, till two months afterwards he quitted her care, cured and healed, and swearing himself her slave for life. She smiled rather absent-mindedly at his expressions of devotion, because an enforced investigation of his effects when he was brought in with his head-wound had shown him to be a married man with a devoted wife the other side of the globe.

When the most critical fighting of that year was over, and an enforced lull had supervened, she obtained a month's leave of absence and revisited her home in the wilds of Herefordshire. Her father's mind was more than before engrossed in the past. So far as his bodily strength and clerical duties permitted, he was tracing Roman roads, which certainly seem to have abounded in Herefordshire and South Wales. Her aunt-housekeeper was distinctly peevish, saying that the west Herefordshire climate provoked rheumatism, and that the dullness of the position reduced her alternately to tears or a desire for frantic violence and a lodging in the Kennington New Road. When would Amethyst—oh, she could not *stomach* abbreviations—a name was a name and not a couple of aimless syllables—when would Amethyst see her way to put aside this war excitement and return to home duties?

Finding that Frederick was not at home, Amy bicycled over to Hathergill Grange. Grace was genuinely pleased to see her, and that rather feckless Betty implored that she might be taken back to France "as a sort of under-nurse, don't you know?"

Grace, becoming confidential, would look at her curiously and say, "Were you astonished at Fred's wedding? *I* was. I always thought you and he were privately engaged. But I suppose it was largely the want of money that led him to marry Ida. . . . She has two thousand a year, dear! Think of that! And when her father dies—and he already suffers from a fatted liver or what ever they call it—she will have four or five thousand a year, perhaps more! I suppose you and Fred agreed when war broke out to go your separate ways? Well—sometimes I feel a little disappointed. I had grown to like you so much, and Fred, before the War, was *such* a cub! . . . Do tell us something of the horrors you have seen. Life here is *so* flat and uninteresting. . . ."

In January, Amy was back at her post in the Amiens hospital. It was a time of lull. Some said our Fifth Army on the Oise would play a great part in the spring campaign, in conjunction with the Americans. The performances of "The Follies" at General Gough's headquarters in Noyon attracted much attention. They were screamingly funny, almost professional in studied drollery. It was considered that the merriment they caused gave our exhausted, anxious men "tone," turned their thoughts for a moment from the horrors ahead. Several of Amy's junior colleagues obtained permission to go to Noyon, but Amy busied herself with something of her old thoroughness, reorganising the hospital, increasing its accommodation, preparing for the worst while hoping for betterment. She was a little surprised inwardly that her thoughts turned so often to Frederick. Why, in 1915, 1916, she had almost ceased to think of him! . . .

In the early part of March she saw in a Herefordshire newspaper "that Colonel and Mrs. Frederick Hathergill had been visiting the Colonel's father at Hathergill Grange, and that Mrs. Hathergill, the bride of the year before, would stay at her father-in-law's house while her husband returned to his command at the Front, his leg being now wholly healed."

Amy's heart leapt, though she tried to convince herself such emotions and reminiscences were beneath her position as head-nurse at a military hospital. Then came a rare letter from Grace: "Fred and Ida had been with them. . . . Fred still more improved and looking so well as a young Colonel and prospective father; for it was an open secret that dear Ida was near the end of her confinement. Alas for the calls of war! Fred's leave could not now be extended further. The poor young wife was in tears every day, convinced she would see him no more. Still—as it had to be—they were positively glad to see the last of him. The baby was expected in two or three months. . . . Old Mrs. Canwell of Robertson's Cottages, at Gresley Common, had literally died of joy—was it not sad?—at the return of her son Oswald, after she had been officially informed three weeks before of his death. It wasn't *her* Oswald, but a stranger or a far-off cousin of the same name. . . ." and so on. . . . At the end was a postscript saying that, Fred's regiment being now at Amiens, Amy might see much more of him than they would for the next twelve months. . . .

Amy felt in reading this what the French would call *toute chose*. However, her duties began once more to be all-absorbing. One side and the other, through February and March, were evidently tightening for the great attack, even though our Fifth Army at Noyon was still interested in theatricals and amateur concerts through the first half of March 1918.

The attack came; the Fifth Army crumpled and fell back—back—back—until at last Amiens had ceased to be tenable in the spreading German pressure. Frederick and Amy had met long before, in the month of March. She had been prepared for seeing him, had schooled herself to be very professional, alert, busy, absent-minded if he spoke of home, and strictly disciplinarian. She called him "Colonel Hathergill." This when on duty was proper, and could not be otherwise. "But was she never *off* duty?" asked Frederick of the air. Never able to slip away for an hour at one time or another, tell him about herself and all that had happened since 1914?

"Never," she answered imperturbably, when one day he impatiently put the question—"never, while these horrors are going on." And she waved a blood-stained hand —she was on her way to wash it—toward more and more convoys slowly approaching the hospital with their loads of wounded.

Amiens became at last untenable. Our forces received orders to retire to the west of it and dig themselves in. Colonel Hathergill became increasingly anxious about the matron of the hospital, Sister Amy. The nurses, patients, and staff had evacuated the place some hours. Amy was not with them. He approached the building at dusk during a lull in the bombardment. His orderly followed.

There must have been disaster to the building after its abandonment. Two shells had entered it. Approach needed caution because of the broken glass in all directions "Amy!" he called, in increasing urgency; "Amy! Amy!" At last he thought he heard a faint answering

FREDERICK'S REMORSE

cry, "Frederick!" He listened, but another roar of distant firing drowned all sound of human voices. He got into the central hall of the building. Its roof was partly smashed, and one star twinkled in the grey-blue opening. Again he shouted, "Amy!" No answer. He scrambled up the still intact stone staircase—one side of it—while his orderly ascended the other. He felt his way into this room and that. His orderly pursued a parallel search. At last he heard him calling, "Here, Colonel, here!"

Amy was lying on the floor of her bedroom, between bed and wall. He entered very gingerly because the flooring was not intact. The bed, save for a fall of dust, was uninjured. His orderly scooped it off, while he himself put his arm gently round the shoulders of the dying woman. The orderly turned the quilt back, and then assisted Colonel Hathergill to lift Sister Amy with the greatest care and lay her on the opened bed. The underside of her was soaked with blood.

She opened her eyes and looked at Frederick with such a full-eyed glow of gratitude and joy as was perceptible even in the dim light from the shattered window. He held her hands, crying as he did so as he had never cried before. The orderly lit a bull's-eye lamp and placed it on the washing-stand, then stumbled, rumbled down the great staircase to summon medical assistance—too late.

SIR MATTHEW CASELY BROMPTON

WHEN Sir Matthew Brompton died a year ago he had been about two years in retirement; and before that, the Great War had distracted every one's attention from the innermost affairs of the Circumlocution Office. But thirty years ago there was considerable excitement for a week over his name, and even his continuance in the public service. Questions in Parliament had been put and cleverly parried. The Leader of the Opposition had damped down his followers' clamour because he really knew all the facts of the case from a private talk with the Minister most concerned.

This was the case as far as I could make it out. Matthew—I always disliked his first name because of its unnecessary deviation in spelling from the Græco-Armaic Mattaios—Matthew Casely Brompton was the eldest, I think the only, son of Matthew Burton Brompton and Cicely Casely. The wearisome name, Matthew, had been an outstanding feature in the Brompton family since the early eighteenth century, and possibly since the Cromwellian period, when the Bromptons of Buckinghamshire sided with Parliament against the King.

From the reign of George the First, however, they had become connected with the Civil Service. A Brompton was clerk to Sir Robert Walpole (nowadays we should call it private secretary); a Brompton had something to

SIR MATTHEW CASELY BROMPTON 149

do with William Pitt; another went rather off the rails in the affairs of Queen Caroline, consort of George IV But another Brompton was a notable personage in the Office of the Duchy of Lancaster—the person who really ran the business in the 'fifties and 'sixties.

It is his son—he married when he was forty-five—who is the "Matthew" of this slight sketch. Picture him doing all that a respectable, comfortably obscure, and secure Civil Servant's son should have done at that period— Rugby, Wadham College, Oxford; and entry—after passing a stiffish examination—into the Circumlocution Office.

He must have got into that Department of State about 1886, and after wrestling uncomplainingly for years with commercial questions on a foundation of Latin and Ancient Greek, Aristotelean Logic and Algebra, he was promoted for his stolid industry to being private secretary to Lord Drossmore, who became Parliamentary Under-Secretary for Circumlocution.

At the time Matthew was about thirty he fell violently in love with Margaret Dupont, one of the Drossmore's four daughters. He had, in fact, never been violent before about anything, and even in this stress of emotion his violence was only relative. It did not affect his daily work in the little room at the end of the long passage in the Circum. Office (as it was playfully called by the junior clerks), but it constrained him to lose no opportunity of meeting Margaret in her home, in such section of society as Matthew could afford to enter, and at houses she visited in the country. If you affected the same centres, you might have there seen or encountered a rather grave-looking, tall young man, wearing spectacles and a scrubby brown moustache, perhaps even, in the very earliest period of this obsession, a little whisker. He would have been determinedly silent on all matters connected with the Circum. Office, or its interest in Foreign and Imperial affairs. But he would have surprised you with his skill at chess, and his passionate interest in languages other than Ancient Greek and Latin of the Augustan period. He knew all about the breaking up of the intolerable Latin of the classics into the lovely Romance languages, and I believe it was he who annonymously translated *Diez's Comparative Grammar* into English.

Margaret Dupont I saw somewhere in the middle 'eighties. She may have been twenty-two at the time. She had three other sisters, younger and older, and they all married well, though quite plain of feature, and had large, wholesome families of good-looking, freckled children. But Margaret was still single at twenty-two; glaringly pretty, pitilessly courageous in hunting and rod-fishing, in shooting and boat-steering, and in costume-wearing in the London season. She was the most giraffe-life in figure of the fashionable young women at the Healtheries or the Colonial and Indian Exhibitions, but it was said that in the hunting field she dared to go without a bustle.

It was also said that she was frantically in love with her impossible Irish cousin, Captain Donagh M'Donagh, of the Eleventh Dragoons. But Donagh, having nothing but his captain's pay and great good looks, and a terribly hearty mode of love-making, was evidently not going to

SIR MATTHEW CASELY BROMPTON

propose to a girl with little more than £2000 down when she did marry.

So Margaret's laugh became louder and harsher, her eyes more and more dazzling, her teeth more glittering, her cheeks rosier, and her hair more purely gold, until she married Matthew in 1891.

After her marriage much less was seen of her. Matthew ceased to be private secretary, being promoted to be head of a department which dealt with pensions (I think). He was well on his way to becoming an Assistant Under-Secretary when the main incident of his life happened.

At three in the morning a surgeon was called into No. 5 Bucklemore Gardens, Iddesleigh Place, to prescribe for a gentleman—Major M'Donagh—who had been very severely wounded by a revolver—three revolver bullets. The house was the residence of Mr. Brompton, a head clerk in an important public office.

Major M'Donagh was almost past speech at the time; still, he averred while he could yet speak, and as far as they could understand him, that the whole thing had been an accident. After a return from the theatre and a little supper, he had been explaining to Mr. Brompton and his wife the workings of the new service revolver, and by some mishandling of the weapon three of its chambers had been discharged.

He died two days afterwards. The Hon. Mrs. Brompton was too prostrated with grief and horror to give any intelligible evidence, and Mr. Brompton's own account of the mishap did not differ much from that of the wounded man.

Verdict: Death from misadventure.

I did not see Matthew for some years afterwards—about the time of King Edward's Coronation. I was a little disappointed at his lessened interest in the Romance languages, but was impressed by his enormous powers of work. Mrs. Brompton I thought badly made-up in complexion, and her incessant chatter and shrieking laugh rather depressed me.

They had two nice children—girls. Brompton was very hard-worked during the last year of the Balfour Administration, and received a well-earned knighthood in 1905, when he became Assistant Under-Secretary. I often asked myself if in later life he had ever known happiness; but I was told he had—in golf—and in his eldest daughter.

"OLD ARTHUR"

IF you know anything of Shropshire—the southern part of it—you know Callers Castle, the Duke of Dumbarton's seat. Its name is pronounced with an *æ* sound to the first vowel, and has nothing to do with the verb "to call." I believe there is a Shropshire dialect word, "to cal," but forget what it means.

"Old Arthur," as he came to be known by his intimates in later years, was in 1889 the college friend—or one of the thirty or forty college friends—at Oxford of Lord Minsterley, the eldest son of Dumbarton's duke. I think his father was a manufacturer of dogs' biscuits in the Midlands, fairly well off, but parent of a very large family. Arthur, the eldest son, wanted to go to Oxford after some success at Shrewsbury Grammar School, so the father sent him. But beyond that his gains with a new patent dog biscuit did but march parallel with his procreation of twelve children; so that he could only assure Arthur—in common with the eleven others—an ultimate income of about £200 a year.

Why the young, handsome, blithe, military-minded Lord Minsterly took up with Arthur as a college friend I cannot tell you; or, rather, I lack the space. One reason no doubt was that Minsterley, beside all his debonair gallantry and interest in weapons, liked dogs, consequently dog biscuits, and therefore thought Arthur interesting.

153

Arthur was—is—interesting, if you know where to look for it; but chiefly in manure research and vegetable chemistry.

Well, Minsterley brought Arthur (whose manufacturing father lived in a bricky part of Staffordshire) down to Callers Castle one Easter just before he, Minsterley, passed away from Oxford to the Guards. Arthur was large, quiet, rather studious, not exactly nice-looking, yet quite personable. The duchess felt straight away she *liked* Arthur—whom they all called "Arthur" on the fourth day of his week's stay—and thought him a far nicer friend for her boy than the preceding introductions from the University. The duke said he was a real sound fellow, and knew a lot about manures that we all ought to know. The girls thought he was rather slow; the younger boys considered him a duffer—but an amiable duffer. That was the general effect of the first visit at Easter.

Arthur came again in September at the duke's invitation—and Minsterley, down for partridge-shooting, was jolly glad to have him there. Arthur shot partridges rather under protest, but, at any rate, knew much that ought to be known about guns. Arthur came again the following Easter because the duchess had heard vaguely good reports of his success at Oxford; the duke liked to talk to him on the chemistry of soils: and Minsterley could not have a steadier friend. . . . Her darling boy had been just a little wild that year (1890) in London. . . .

At Callers Castle—where now you may smoke anywhere—there were still in the year of the great African

"OLD ARTHUR"

agreement with Germany (of which the duke approved in the House of Lords) two smoking-rooms, in those days a generous allowance. One was very large and long, and contained the fullest-possible-sized billiard-table, seats in tiers along its sides, cupboards containing all manner of games and liqueurs and biscuits and sweets, and shelves of boys' books. Beyond that, again, in a terminal sense was the second smoking-room, an addition built out in the 'seventies. This ended in a good deal of glass, but had two or more most comfortable sofas, several capacious arm-chairs, and a large fireplace. . . . Heaps and *heaps* of books ranged along the walls. *Now* it has a discreet side door leading down through wiggly-waggly stone steps into some domain of the butler's. But in 1890 it still only communicated lawfully with the rest of the castle by the door leading into the billiard-room.

Here Arthur was wont to resort—usually alone, while the others played billiards or pool, or fooled about. One night on his third visit the younger members of the party, a little piqued by his studies of chemical manures (there was a great concourse of books and pamphlets on this subject, a favourite one of the agricultural-minded duke, in the outer library's shelves), whispered that it would be an awful lark to lock "old Arthur" in. So they did, from the billiard-room side, and went up to bed. Minsterley, who would have thought this "dam' silly," was at the other side of the house—conservatories—flirting with an extremely nice girl whom he afterwards married.

Arthur had, as a matter of fact, lain down on one of the deliciously comfortable, very capacious sofas near the fireplace to read a book on vegetable manures. It may be he dropped off to sleep over the fascinating account it gave of the devious habits of broad beans under varying stimuli. He woke up, however, looked at his watch, saw it was 11:15, rose, shook himself, and made for the door leading into the billiard-room. But the door was locked on the farther side. It was no use rattling the handles; the absence of any light-gleam, the silence, told him every one on the other side had gone up to bed, leaving him locked into the smoking-room library. He glanced at the three great windows clustered round the fireplace end. Could he get out on to any roof projection below? And creep along to some kitchen or front-door entrance and get let in? He might, of course—it was physically possible, but also it would very likely result in spraining this or that, damaging the roof or his own person. Then there might be watch-dogs. . . .

No; it was better to accept his fate, take a bearskin rug as a cover, and sleep near the fire on one of the exquisitely comfortable sofas. He did so. . . . Some hour or so later he awoke. . . . . What was that noise? It—was —some one—skilfully—unlocking a window from the outside ledge—opening it—and descending cautiously into the room. From his sofa Arthur peered out with one eye and saw a dark figure in silhouette against a glare from some primitive electric lantern, such as they used down in the mines. Suspecting the next turn would be in his direction, he wisely kept his head under the ample bearskin—and suddenly the light flashed on his sofa. Fortunately it only rested there a very short time, and whisked round to the central door on the other side. The holder of the lantern made for that; in less than a minute, with some adroit tool he had pushed back the ward of the lock and passed into the billiard-room, and was flashing his light round the walls.

Then he had opened the billiard-room door and was making, through another sitting-room, for the great hall of the castle where treasures of considerable value, shown to the public once a week, lay behind cut-glass and locks deemed foolishly to be unpickable. Arthur acted perhaps eccentrically, and by instinct. He closed the door of his room very quietly. The lock was disgruntled. He placed against its opening inward such articles of furniture as he could move.

Then—with open windows—he started a hell of a row. . . . *"Stop thief!" "Wake up!" "Burglars in the hall!"* He banged fire-irons, he clanged trays. After that he made for the open window where the thief had entered, taking the bearskin from the sofa. This he flung out on to the stone pavement below and dropped on to it. Catching up the rug again, he scrambled through doorways with picked locks, and past a dead—poisoned—watchdog, on to the lawn in front of the great house, and only paused for breath and deliberation in a shady recess outside the great entrance. As he did so he heard a vague inside clamour, and saw the massive hall door quietly and gently open, and a figure slithering out with things under its left arm. As it passed where he stood he flung at it, and over it, the great bearskin, and following up the impact of the rug, bore this figure to the gravel, shouting as loudly as he could.

The legs tried to kick him, but could not reach his ample body, as he sat on the man's chest. The arms of the prostrate person were enclosed in the rug; moreover, one arm still held a gold clock and a silver vase. . . .

Scarcely more than a minute passed, and through the hall door, flung widely open, out into the moonlight came the groom of the chambers (as he believed the super-butler to be called), the duke in a dressing-gown, Lord Ministerly in pyjamas and a blazer, two footmen in trousers and shirts, and the second boy of the house, wearing very little.

The burglar—a stout, well-shaped young man from Wolverhampton—an engineer out of employment . . . it was just before the days of the safety bicycle or the great extension of steam engines, when all engineers became honourably employed or worked off their wickedness bicycling—the burglar was tried and sentenced to five years' penal servitude.

What to do with "old Arthur" did not long perplex the duke's mind. "You must leave Oxford," he said the next morning, when the police had taken away the half-asphyxiated burglar—"leave Oxford, my dear chap, and work for me. . . . You're *made* for the estate, with your knowledge of manures and chemistry, and I've liked you from the moment I set eyes on you a year ago."

Arthur had equally fallen in love with Callers Castle and its estate. Old Milburd, the head agent, now seventy-one, retired in 1892 on a pension, and Arthur, who had worked under him nearly two years, succeeded to his position.

"OLD ARTHUR"

To make "old Arthur" happy, there only remained one other achievement—to marry the Lady Muriel, the duke's second daughter.

Muriel was in '92 a shapely girl of twenty-one, with a good figure and clear skin, but she had nothing like the beauty of her sisters; her hair was rather short (which wouldn't have mattered nowadays), she had no musical talent, and was a little clumsy at field games or in dancing. But she was intensely fond of gardening, and even of botany—predilections which drew her much into her father's company and "old Arthur's." You respected her in the composition of phosphatic manures which changed the colour of geraniums, though you merely felt pityingly kind if you met her at Buckingham Palace or at Prince's Skating Club. Her laugh was not a musical one.

But to Arthur, almost from his taking up the agency, she had seemed wholly delightful. Nevertheless, she refused him—quite nicely—when he ventured to propose (in 1894), yet continued to work much in his company. . . . He asked her again in 1895, but, though tearful and very charming, she said they—must—live—their—lives —out—separately—and—and—— She forgot the other prepared sentences—and fell on his covert-coat in tears— and accepted him.

Old Arthur in the succeeding years, besides a large family, had such astounding success in Shropshire with his chemical manures that each Minister in succession fled the Duke of Dumbarton, who could talk of nothing else, with the concurrent assumption that "old Arthur" must get a knighthood. But Lord Salisbury, being himself a great chemist, succumbed to these representations in 1901, and Muriel, the wife of the distinguished agricultural chemist, Sir Arthur Brownbank, no longer feels the least jealous of her sisters, who all espoused peers.

As to the burglar, I may tell you later on what happened to him.

SAMUEL GWILLYM

EARLY in 1895, an ex-convict, named S. G. (Samuel Gwillym) Brown, left Portland prison for South Africa. He was aged twenty-nine—approximately—and had been serving a sentence of five years' penal servitude (reduced by a few months owing to good conduct) for a burglary at Callers Castle, the seat of the Duke of Dumbarton, in the south of Shropshire. His capture there was mainly due to the duke's agent, Mr. Arthur Brownbank, an important witness at the trial.

Some time after his conviction, however, Mr. Brownbank obtained permission to see the convict in prison. "I hear," he said, " you are behaving very well. If so, you are reducing your term of imprisonment by a few months. I judge people mainly by their faces. I did not see much of yours when you were burgling the duke's castle—naturally—or you might have damaged mine. But I watched you a good deal during your trial, and somehow I cannot believe you are naturally bad or will not pull yourself together in some other land when your sentence has expired. Continue to do well during the term of hard labour; then when you come out, let me know—same address—I am the duke's agent now—and I will see if I can give you a helping hand."

Years passed, and at length, in February 1895, Mr.

Brownbank received a letter from the ex-convict, and in reply furnished him with a third-class passage to Cape Town, a letter of introduction to a Guano company having its headquarters there, and a credit note on a South African bank of £50, to be paid at any office of the said bank in Cape Colony.

The result was that Brown was engaged by this Guano company for a term of three years, subject to good behaviour, and sent to Ichaboe Island, nearly opposite Lüderitz Bay (Angra Pequena), in German South-West Africa. Lüderitz Bay and all the coast between the Orange River on the south and the Kunene River on the north was German after 1885, but seven small guano islands off the coast (together with Walvisch Bay) remained British. The islands (uninhabited except by agents of the Guano company) belonged to this association, which exported the massed accumulations of seabird's droppings that had fallen on these rocks for untold ages. They were manufactured, of course, into guano manure.

Unless you were interested in bird life, in the constant spectacle of immense sea waves from the Antartic Ocean dashing into foam against pitiless rocks on an unprotected coast, life under these conditions, which S. G. Brown had to face, must have been pretty ghastly, and the stench of the dug guano sickening in its cumulative effects.

Every now and then, of course, he got a few days or even a week off, and had himself rowed by two Cape boys to the mainland (if the sea were not too rough), and there spent the holidays looking about him. For the first year, being on trial, and the Guano company having some knowledge of his past, he got little more pay than was just pocket money, and rations of food landed every month or so by the guano-collecting steamer. In the second year, at much higher pay, he was transferred to Hollam's Bird Island, farther north. This as a residence was terribly dreary to any one but an ornithologist; and even an ornithologist might be weary after a couple of months of the society of gannets, cormorants, gulls, petrels, and penguins. On the opposite shore there were only uninhabited sandhills.

But the guano-collecting boats brought him literature of a sort, and newspapers; he had a few Cape boys and Hottentots with him; and with the hot sun and bellowing ocean breezes he grew strong and very vigorous. He wrote about twice a year to Mr. Brownbank, reiterating his gratitude for this new opening in life, but saying several times that when the three years of his engagement were completed he should make for the mainland and try his luck among the Germans.

From Ichaboe he had once landed and marched for two days up a dry river-bed which had some very promising indications; and from Hollam's Bird Island he had on a week's holiday penetrated inland to the Ganin plateau —among the Ganin bushmen. Thereafter his communications ceased. The Guano company wrote favourably about him, but said the day after his engagement expired —he was then at Possession Island—he had left their employment, and had passed over to Niederlassung, the German station on Lüderitz Bay.

Twelve years must have passed by, during which

Arthur Brownbank ("Sir Arthur," after 1901) would almost have forgotten having interested himself in the fate of S. G. Brown. One day in—I think it was 1911, the very hot year with a wonderful summer—he received a letter at his Shropshire office (Clunbury) signed "Samuel Gwillym," saying the writer, once of his acquaintance and recently back from South Africa, would like to call upon him one day soon whilst staying at the Red Lion Hotel, New Radnor. At whatever hour was convenient to Sir Arthur Brownbank, the writer would motor over.

"Gwillym?—Samuel Gwillym?" Welsh, of course, but the surname conveyed nothing to Sir Arthur's remembrance. The estate had a good deal to do with Wales in these later times, the duke having sold all his Dumbarton property to the town of Glasgow, and put much of his money into Welsh land near the Shropshire border. Perhaps this man wished to buy some of the Radnorshire land. Both the duke and Brownbank anticipated a boom in that direction—one of the loveliest counties in the three kingdoms. Brownbank therefore dictated a curt answer to the letter, fixing a day and hour for him to call at the Clunbury office. On this day, at that time, he was announced: "Mr. Gwillym." Arthur, as he faced him, saw a stoutly built, hard-bitten, very tanned, rather scarred, rather too well-dressed man—of—of—well, he would guess him to be between forty and fifty—rather nearer fifty. The face might, indeed, have said that age, but the eyes were young looking. As they met *his* eyes, fair and square, and twinkled—an inspiration—a remembrance—S. G. Brown, as he had last seen him in his cell

SAMUEL GWILLYM

at Portland prison. It was—it *must* be—S. G. Brown. And, of course, Brown's second name had been Gwillym, or something like it, and he had been partly Welsh.

Arthur's eyes conveyed recognition of the past to Mr. Gwillym, but Arthur's tongue—his secretary being within hail—just said, "Sit down, Mr. Gwillym. You wanted, I think, to see me about some farmstead of the duke's in Radnorshire?" Then he got up and closed the door leading into the clerks' office.

"I did. I see, in spite of the lapse of time, you recognise me. My name *is* Gwillym, remember; but—but—I should much like to shake hands with you. We won't talk about the past, the far past yet awhile—at any rate; but may I shake hands? You were very good to me, years ago, and I think I can show you I have done well for myself."

Arthur at once extended his right hand. Gwillym gripped it firmly. Then puffed out exhausted air as he sat down, dabbed his forehead a little with a silk handkerchief, and said, "Whew! But it *is* hot! Partly the weather— and I always thought England was so dam' chilly, in days gone by. But I've been motoring, and— well, you know, Sir Arthur, I rather had to screw myself up to this. I couldn't write much—never knew who might read my letters. 'Sides, I wasn't going to write till I'd made a devil of a lot of money, and could come back here and settle down for the rest of my days. Now I want to see you about this little place near New Radnor. These are the particulars," and he put a newspaper advertisement before Brownbank, on his desk, "and here is a reference to my bankers in London—letter from them—

just to show you I've got the funds. Don't mind tellin' you, in fact, I've got seventy-five thou. placed at that bank. Still more, don't mind tellin' you every detail as to how I got it—honest—for your own ear only, of course. You know—or rather you don't know—that after I quitted that guano-collecting business I was out in the hunt after diamonds in German South-West. Somehow I always hit it off with the natives—dam' sight better than with some of the white men. Ah! I've had some stiff times, *I* can tell you! Well, one of the Hottentots I had under me used to tell me of the stones his people had found near this Ganin plateau—side towards the sea. So when I got free of my contract I went off with him. We had a devil of a time—found nothing at first, though I made a bit of money over other things. Married a German missionary's daughter in 1901—name of Anna, but always called her 'Annie.' Real good sort she is. Best woman ever I met. Don't know a word, of course, about what brought me out to Africa, just thought I got into some trouble with my Government. Then in nineteen eight, nineteen nine, I struck it *rich*. It was I that found the "German Empress" diamond, say what you like. Had a bit of a quarrel over it, but justice in the long run. Got three-quarters of the sale money. . . . And then others. But I wasn't out for too much. When I saw my way to realising between seventy and eighty thousand pounds, says I to me wife, 'We'll turn all this into money and make for England. Buy a little place there and live out the rest of our lives real happy, doin' no harm to any one, and nobody wantin' to do harm to us.' So here I am!"

SAMUEL GWILLYM

"I'm really interested to hear this," said Arthur, thinking hard. "I'll tell you what. You've come in a motor? I've got to finish some business here with my clerks before I go to lunch. It's now twelve-thirty, or nearly so. You go a turn or two round about and come back here at *one*. Then we'll both start off—I must take the estate motor—for Callers Castle, and have lunch together and a talk. Only my wife is there. The duke and duchess are in London, my own house is having something done to it, and my wife and I are staying in her old home—often do. We shall be quite alone after lunch, and you can finish telling me about your life in South Africa—ah! and finish it in the room where we first met."

Samuel Gwillym made an inarticulate noise which novelists would describe as a chuckle, and went out. Arthur glanced from the window and saw him move away in the motor. Then he touched a handbell. A clerk came in. "Edwards! Telephoning through to London is seldom any good on this rotten 'phone. Answers too faint. But telephone to our agents at Bristol and ask *them, pretty briskly,* to get on to the 'phone address of the British South African Bank in London and inquire if they have a client on their books: SAMUEL GWILLYM. Here's the name—GWILLYM. He's come to England from Cape Town—recently. I want to know if he has a considerable sum of money there to his credit. He has given them as a reference. Twig?"

The clerk set about this. Arthur himself telephoned to Lady Muriel to say he was bringing a guest back to lunch —might not be there till 1.45.

The clerk after a long course of bell-ringing and distant

vocal clamour and subdued oaths came back with the reply from the London bank that a gentleman of the name given, with South African recommendations, had deposited a large sum at their head office in London. He was at present on a motoring tour in Wales—Radnorshire, they thought.

At one o'clock punctually Mr. Gwillym returned and sat in the waiting-room below. Arthur joined him, and the two motors went off to Callers Castle.

After lunch Gwillym was taken by Arthur to the smoking-room library beyond the billiard-room. They sat on the deliciously comfortable sofas. "Ah," said Gwillym, "it was here, was it? Lord! to think of my getting in through that window after climbing up to the roof outside. Why, it's a regular music-hall stunt! Couldn't do such a thing nowadays to save me life! And you was" (his grammar was occasionally a little faulty)—"you was a-lyin' under a bearskin on that sofa, and *I* never twigged you! We won't ever refer to it again. Forget it all! But it's worth—*all*—I've bin through since—worth it ALL—and I've had some sickening times to fight through—worth it ALL, to know now I'm an honest man, and you can sit down to a meal with me. . . . Now we might call for my motor, if you don't mind, 'cos you're a busy man, and I ain't one to waste time. I'll be off to the old lady and the children at New Radnor, and tell her I've closed for the place I've hankered after. . . ."

JEANNETTE SIDEBOTHAM

PICTURE to yourself, firstly, a notable mill about a mile south-west of Hornsea in Yorkshire, close to the reedy shores of a mere with many swans and wild duck. Here lived a wealthy miller, and with him as child and young woman his granddaughter, Jeannette Sidebotham.

Old Mr. Sidebotham was said to have come from the wolds of the East Riding, where there were several noteworthy interrelated farming families: the Ramsbothams, the Winterbottoms, the Ecclesbothams, and the Higginbottoms, which took their surnames in the Middle Ages from the sheltered "bottoms" in the wolds where their sheep grazed in safety. Sidebotham's father before him had migrated eastward to the mill on the north shore of Hornsea Mere—his contemporaries said because of his interest in the smuggling business. During the Napoleonic Wars, smuggling craft would come across from Holland, Flanders, and Oldenburg into Bridlington ("Burlington") Bay and slip down to Hornsea in the darkness, land their cargo on the flat shore, and convey it to the ample premises of the mill, a mile inland from the sea, and close to the convenient reedy mystery of the mere.

Free Trade had killed the taste for smuggling long before our Mr. Sidebotham succeeded his father as a miller. Yet there was always a sense of mystery about him, and he was a cranky man who lived aloof from the Hornsea folk. His wife had died soon after the birth of her second child. The elder of the two sons was Jeannette's father. The younger had migrated to America when he was twenty-two, after a quarrel with his father; and there, for the purposes of this story, was the end of him.

The elder son by some contrariety of disposition grew up good, pious, clear-minded, kind-mannered, but of delicate health tending to "consumption." He did not in the least want to be a miller. He was sent to a boarding school after his mother's death, at Bridlington, and afterwards to a college at Hull. Like most young men of a consumptive tendency, he easily fell in love. He also wished to enter the service of the Established Church. This required, however, more education than his father was willing to pay for; but the father did not frown on his idea of marrying when he was only twenty-three, hoping it might "make a man of him." However, he did not become a Congregational minister till he was twenty-five, and he married at the same age, after his wilder, younger brother had left home for America. His father, then, rather scared by the departure of the other son, made the elder a yearly allowance of a hundred pounds, hoping it might serve to establish his health.

His bride had been a school teacher, also rather delicate in constitution. A year after their marriage she gave birth to a little girl, whom she named Jane, after her mother, but "Jane," out of affection and wistfulness, soon lengthened into Janey or Janet. When Jane was three years old her father died of galloping consumption, and the widow and child went to live with the harsh, silent old grandfather at the mill.

Janet grew up a sage, quiet, freckled, whity-brown little thing, on the borderline of prettiness. She was very eager to learn, timidly anxious to find a profession which would maintain her by her own earnings, and much influenced by the story of Jane Eyre. So by the time she was eighteen she had acquired a surprising amount of knowledge from classes faithfully attended at Hull. Spurred on by a still more enterprising comrade of the classes, she jointly answered an advertisement in a scholastic paper asking for English teachers in a school near Brussels. They were both accepted, after correspondence, with board, lodging, and a salary to start at of £25 a year. Janet's grandfather growled somewhat, her mother bleated and pleaded her own impaired health, but Janet was pleasantly, submissively firm, and the two young women, with palpitating hearts, went to Goole or some such place, steamered to Antwerp, and thence travelled by train to the school at Vilvoorden.

No; it was not—as you are about to imagine—a trick of the White Slave traffic to secure recruits, but quite an honest girls' school, with kind, practical teachers; and Jeannette—as she now called herself—became positively happy there, and after six months spoke French quite fluently, with a Belgian pronunciation. She even learnt a little Flemish. Her surname ceased to trouble her. "Sidé-botham," it was carefully pronounced. No one in Belgium dreamt of nudging any one else as they named her, which was what they were inclined to do round Hull, unless their own names were Sidebotham, Winterbottom,

Ramsbotham, or Higginbottom. Jeannette remained at this school for three years, with one brief holiday at Hornsea Mill. In the last year of her stay her friend married a Belgian, and she took over her classes and was promoted to a salary of £50 a year. There was a prospect of a further rise, but just after her twenty-first birthday came a letter from her grandfather telling her in a few phrases that her mother was dying of anæmia and complications.

She returned. Her mother died. Her grandfather then insisted she should stay and housekeep for him. If she refused, he would have nothing more to do with her, and would leave his money to an institution.

More from a sense of duty than any thought about his few thousands of pounds, she remained—and the Great War broke out. Jeannette learnt to housekeep on the allowance he gave; she proffered her services for warwork in various directions not too far away, instancing her knowledge of French. But three great ladies in that part of Yorkshire also thought they knew French, and their services were accepted in preference to hers. So in reality she had little war-work offered her, and after her housewifely tasks were done, with the aid of their general servant, she spent much of her time in a punt on the lake, reading books. Occasionally they had the scare of an air-raid from Germany; but the air-raiders were not inclined to waste their bombs on such an inconsiderable place as Hornsea; they were aiming at Hull and the big industrial cities farther inland.

Jeannette and her grandfather got quite used to seeing in the early morning or the sunny evening German aircraft—Fokkers, even Zeppelins—passing overhead to ravage the Midlands and the manufacturing towns, or else returning towards the North Sea, sometimes pursued by our own aeroplanes.

There had been a big air-raid on the Hull region in early June, 1918. The Sidebothams' servant had seen the machines, like brilliant specks in the sky, as she dressed in the morning light. Jeannette, after the morning's household duties were over, went for a walk along the shore of the mere. Presently she encountered near the waterside a stranded Fokker plane, and inspected it curiously. It was scarcely damaged, but did not seem to be English; the black Maltese cross in its details proclaimed it German. Yet it was apparently abandoned. What should she do? At once inform the authorities at Hornsea and have a small army of tramplers come out to wander about their grounds and utterly spoil the quiet beauty of the lake shore and break down the reed clumps coming into blossom? While she pondered there came a voice from the sketching-booth she had erected with her own hands—reeds and sticks and a bit of sailcloth—hard by; a place where she might either read or sketch, protected from the summer sun. The voice somehow did not frighten her; it was talking French, and she loved the sound of the French language. It could not be a German who was speaking because the accent was so "Belgian," only differing from "French" French by the aspiration of the *h*. The speaker added a further appeal: "Mademoiselle, ayez pitié! Je suis meurtri de ma chute! Je m'en meurs!"

She walked to the reed shelter, trembling with excitement and apprehension, and saw within it, rather hunched up, a good-looking young man in a German air uniform. "Qui etes vous?" she asked rather aimlessly. He poured forth a story in French, and it thrilled her to find how well she understood him. He was a native of Malmédy close to the Belgian frontier, but a small northern portion of the "Walloon" country which had somehow been incorporated for a hundred years or more in Prussian territory. He told her that he and his spoke French—or rather, Walloon—in their own home, but, being a German subject, he had been obliged to take part in the War. His profession was piano-tuning; therefore, with some appropriateness he had been trained in an Air Corps, had indeed shown no opposition to this since it might provide him with a means of escape. So he had taken part in this last air-raid, hoping to descend somewhere in safety and give himself up to an enemy, whom, if allied to France or Belgium, he could not regard as a foe. Holland showed no sympathy with Belgium in any way, especially over the Walloon country . . . otherwise. . . . For himself, he had been serving with the Air Corps at Ghent. . . .

Jeannette listened to this flood of explanation; then suggested that the speaker should endeavour to limp by her side to the Mill House, where she would confer with her grandfather, and where he should certainly have a meal—for he was very hungry. He staggered to his feet; he thought his right leg had been strained, but the limp had almost passed away as he walked, supported by her arm.

At the Mill House Jeannette put him in the sitting-room

to eat a meal—a forestallment of their dinner—while she went in search of her grandfather. The latter was not much disposed to sympathise with the young man, being much annoyed that the Fokker machine should have landed on his ground. Its presence there would bring a crowd of idle and thievish sightseers and excursionists. He insisted that Jeannette should go in that very afternoon to Hornsea with the man and give him up. So, quite willingly, after a hearty lunch, the airman accompanied her, she driving him there in their gig, and he was handed over to the coastguard pending a more military authority.

But even when the latter had taken him over, as no one amongst them could speak French or German, Jeannette was politely sent for to interpret. The Walloon soldier gave his name as François Oudler, but admitted that in the shreds of identification papers which he handed over he was written down "Franz." He held the rank of unter-offizier in the German Army. . . . Had always been unwilling to serve, but could not help himself. . . . Was by profession a musician and piano-tuner. . . . Had relations on Belgian territory, as well as in Germany. . . .

He was at first interned near Hull, but the good impression he had made was extended. In the pursuit of his father's musicshop business in Malmédy he had travelled much in the Liége country as well as in the Rhenish Province. He explained the eagerness of his fellow-countrymen of this French-speaking strip to be joined to the rest of the Walloon population in Eastern Belgium when the War was over—if the Allies conquered. He was, after a month or two, especially when great triumphs were coming to us in France, and victory seemed assured, let out on parole to confer with officers of the Intelligence Division. . . . His internment at last became almost nominal. . . . There were journeys to London and back. . . .

Yet he continued to see much of Jeannette, though he no longer pronounced her surname Sidé-botham, but Saïd-bossom. . . . It was generally considered in her neighbourhood that he, being—as they phrased it—"as good as a Belgian," would get married to Jeannette after the War, the end of which, in late October, seemed suddenly close. When the Armistice was signed, the future Belgian citizenship of François was assumed. At any rate, he was released under some formula or other and sent to Liége to join the British forces as an interpreter and a person well acquainted with the local conditions of the Rhenish Province bordering on Liége. He had been excessively polite, touchingly grateful to Jeannette—everything but a lover. But she attributed his reticence to delicacy of mind. . . . He could not speak of his heart's emotions, she felt, while his nationality was German, and before the readjustment of frontiers.

He had left her after a respectfully tender farewell in November 1918, to join the British Army marching on Cologne; for by this time he spoke English quite well, in addition to his German, his Rhenish *kanderwalsch,* his Walloon dialect, and Belgian French— left her convinced that in a month or two he would implore her to marry him . . . and the only condition she would make would be that this union must entail residence in England or Belgium; otherwise she could not *possibly* consent.

In two months—or, strictly speaking, just after Christmas—a bulky letter from him did arrive, posted at Düren. He informed her that, thanks to the divine goodness of her intervention, he was now restored to his province, had been of great service to the English troops, the Belgian annexation of the Malmédy country was assured, and that soon after the New Year he—here Jeannette had to turn the page—he would wed his cousin, Mlle. Yolande Thioncourt, to whom he had been affianced ever since the beginning of the War. His beloved Yolande had written a note—which he enclosed—protesting her never-to-be-effaced gratitude towards Mlle. Jeannette Sidé-botham.

MRS. MUGGRIDGE

HER maiden surname was Streatfield, but her Christian name was Adela—rather unusual for her station in life, but her mother had been a lady's maid to the Countess of Corquodale (one of whose names was Adela), and had afterwards married a small farmer. She desired to commemorate a kind mistress in the naming of her eldest girl.

Adela was her second child, and, of course, at home was called Addie. When she was twenty-two, and an admirable dairywoman, Harry Muggridge, who was twenty-seven and just starting on his own as a farmer in Somersetshire (by birth he was a Wiltshire man), asked her to marry him. Her mother thankfully assented, as she had four other daughters coming on and growing up.

Muggridge's father had died, and with the £2,000 he inherited, Harry, his third son, thought he, too, would farm. He had a brother in the Navy and a brother in the Army, and a sickly brother who was trying to be a schoolmaster; also two sisters, one of whom had a club-foot and stayed at home with the mother, while the other had married the keeper of the general shop at Puddlingstone and become a little shrewish in disposition.

But the parent Muggridge must have done pretty well out of his large farm (a leasehold), since he left enough

MRS. MUGGRIDGE

money to provide £4,000 for his widow and £2,000 each for his six children. The unexpired lease of the farm sold for £350, which covered the lawyers' expenses, funeral rites, and other small outlay. Harry, in addition, through the absence of the two brothers, carried off most of the farming implements and machinery, poultry, cattle, and horses; while his would-be teacher brother seized most of the books and divided the furniture with the mother and daughters.

The two brothers abroad were promised a valuation and an equivalent, but probably never got either or bothered to ask; one was killed in an Indian frontier war, and the other died of malarial fever on the East Coast of Africa. The soldier left a widow, who, of course, inherited his £2,000. The petty officer had neither married nor left any discoverable will; so after a great deal of delay—several years—his £2,000 was divided between his mother, his eldest brother's widow, his farmer brother, his youngest brother, and his two sisters, working out at about £280 apiece.

But this welcome sum did not come to hand till after Harry had been married four years, and was already feeling anxious, "tight" about money; £2,000 from which to complete the stocking of a sixty-five-acre farm, to pay for rent, labour, food, clothes, grain, and doctors' bills before counter-payments came in, did not seem a great stay against bankruptcy. Harry worked strenuously hard, but Addie for the first four years of her marriage was too much occupied and disqualified by producing three children, a girl and two boys, to do much housework. They had to employ his carter's wife to do much of the cooking and housework. But her husband was proud of his good looks and physical strength, and confident that all would turn out right in the long run. He had had his hand told at Bruton Fair by a palmist in a tent, and she had promised him good fortune through a love affair, and this, said Adela, meant his marriage.

Of course, he had had a village education, which ignored the problems of the field and furrow. He had learnt a deal about the Bible and the life of the Jews in Palestine between 1000 and 200 B.C. and A.D. 2 and 70. He knew a fair amount of arithmetic; had mastered the spelling of English; wrote a readable, facile hand; and retained some vague ideas of English history. He certainly knew the Romans had once ruled England, just as they were the crucifiers of Christ and the originators of the popes and of Queen Mary's religious outrages. His knowledge of farriery (considerable), corn, root crops, ploughing, ditching, and draining was not drawn from books. It owed absolutely nothing to schooling, but had descended from a mouth to mouth and experience to experience from the Latest Stone Age. His father had shown him, and *his* father had learnt what *he* knew about farming from his great-uncle, and so on.

But he was a man of pleasant address and some ambition, and not at all too proud to ask questions and register the answers, or too stupid to read articles and profit by book-learning after he had left the village church school.

His sixty-five-acre farm, which after about four years' anxious struggle was just beginning to pay a small profit,

MRS. MUGGRIDGE

was part of the domain of the East Champney estate, belonging to Lady Judith (Giuditta) Cristadelfini. Lady Judith was one of the many daughters of the Catholic Earl of Porlock, whose family, through religious troubles, had hesitated for two centuries between Italy and England, establishing households in both countries. Giuditta had been stressed into marrying a papalino nobleman of Rome belonging to one of the two or three immensely rich families who had banking houses. Out of the sum he settled on her she had bought back an old family property round East Champney, and, coming there first in the autumn for fox-hunting, now spent an increasing proportion of the year in its leafy solitudes.

She met Harry Muggridge in the huntingfield one day, about four years after his marriage to Adela, and eight years after her own childless union with Count "Bobo" Cristadelfini. She asked him to come and inspect the Home Farm and give her some idea of how it might be developed. He came, and tendered pretty sound advice of a homely kind. Later in the next year she got rid—pleasantly—of old Jargins, her bailiff, and gave the post to Harry, allowing him to continue to live at Grey Mullins, his sixty-five-acre farm.

The schoolmaster brother, having found school-teaching bad for his health, gave it up, and came to live at Grey Mullins with Harry and his wife. In course of time he became uncommonly shrewd over farming—the chemistry part—and got well and strong, so that he, too, married. Then he was turned over by his brother to manage another part of the estate, and dwelt in an enlarged and adapted keeper's cottage. Lady Judith, of course, was known in Roman Italy as la Contessa Cristadelfini. It was only in Somersetshire that they called her "Lady Judith." Some of the farming folk went so far as to call her "Lady Judith Crystal." Harry had great difficulty in mastering her name, but she was quite content to be known in England as "Lady Judith." To every one's surprise she gave birth (in Rome) to a charming boy baby, which she insisted on calling "Arrigo," a common variant of "Enrico" in Italy. But there had been Arrighi in the earlier history of the Cristadelfini family; so the Principe del Palatino, her husband's father, raised no objection.

When her baby was six months old she brought him to England, and the comely, buxom Mrs. Muggridge took a great interest in the child. She, herself, had not only recovered vigour, but had had a fourth child, a little boy, and although she possessed too much instinctive good manners to say such a thing to the Countess, she thought the two babies equally beautiful and extraordinarily alike. Countess "Bobo" a year or two later had one other son, which she named after her husband—Bobadiglia. But she called him "Bobo" for short. He resembled strikingly his elder brother, and, like him, promised to grow up into an excellent type of the modern Roman aristocracy.

Mrs. Muggridge had six children in all. Her eldest boy, Harry, an exceptionally fine young fellow, was killed in the Great War. It was the one lasting grief of her life and of her husband's memory. But she has two valiant daughters and three stout sons likely to do well in the farming line. Her husband manages the whole of the Principessa Palatino's estate in Somersetshire to every one's satisfaction, and the Principe and she spend nearly half the year there. She still hunts, and for that reason comes to England in the late summer and stays here over Christmas.

LADY ISOBEL DRUMHAVEN

ABOUT forty years ago it was thought a little daring, and bordering on the original, to call a girl baby "Isobel." Evelyn and Esmé inspired uncertainty as to sex, there was a wane in Dianas, and a hesitation over Gwladys as leading to disastrous misspelling in tradesmen's accounts. So this idiotic name (Isobel) was given to the second girl of the Crespenhams.

It was a perverse misspelling of "Isabel," and Isabel is merely the Spanish "Ysabel," a decrepit, mediæval pronunciation of Elizabeth.

Well, the Crespenham couple in course of time became Lord and Lady Draxham, and finally the Earl and Countess of Stradlemore. Isobel's elders in the family were (1) the eldest son, Lord Draxham; (2) the Lady Gwendolen Crespenham; (3) the Hon. Frank Crespenham. Then came Isobel, and because her parents lived far back in the nineteenth century, were healthy and nicely simple-minded, they had four more children after her—Mirabel, Jocelyn, Carinthia, and Cuthbert—who compromised by calling their elder sister "Izzo," as though she were a patent poultry food.

Isobel must have been born in 1879, because she was twenty-one in the second year of the South African War. When she was sixteen she managed, very conspicuously, to be in a box at the Alhambra on the occasion (I think)

LADY ISOBEL DRUMHAVEN

when some one recited Alfred Austin's poem on the Jameson Raid. She was with her governess, her eldest brother, and his fiancée. The fiancée was a very nice girl of quite good family. The governess, of course, served as chaperon. Still . . . the Alhambra! And Lord Stradlemore was too severe a Tory (or too cold a Liberal —I forget which) to approve of Rhodes and Jameson. So the poor governess, a clergyman's daughter who tried to be original, was politely sent away and had to go on the stage. Here she played secondary parts, and was too old to attract the bestowers of questionable positions.

In 1896 and 1897 Isobel was, with great difficulty, kept under control and in respectable quietude. She was certainly good-looking. "Positively fetching" was the then new phrase. She read omnivorously in French and English, and in Russian books translated into French. No governess remained with her more than three months, so Miss Burgess's discomfiture in 1896 became annulled. Isobel, when she was twenty-one, came into a thousand a year under her godmother's will. She took Miss Burgess off the stage, as her companion, and started off to South Africa to see the war at as close quarters as Kitchener would allow.

Of course her ostensible society explanation was an invitation to stay at Government House or at Grootschuur, or something of that kind, with her former governess as chaperon. But her intention was to get as near the scenes of fighting as possible, and be a war correspondent for a woman's newspaper.

Everything connected with modern wars is incredible; so you will spare me any deprecatory phrase when I tell you that she and the governess—the governess very battered, Lady Isobel in the pink of freshness and appropriate clothing—actually interviewed Lord Kitchener somewhere in the Orange State, and answered his kindly recommendation to retire to Stellenbosch or England by going in a Cape cart to Pretoria!

Ronald Drumhaven, on Kitchener's staff, fell in love with her daring, her slim figure, her boyish good looks, and followed her to Pretoria, where she had become a great favourite with Lord Roberts, and there outstayed his leave from Kitchener when he married her at the Regimental Church (service conducted by the Bishop of Pretoria). So, although Lord Roberts intervened and obtained a month's leave for his honeymoon, at the end of that month Ronnie had to rejoin his regiment in the northern Transvaal, and was killed in November, 1901.

Ronald Drumhaven was the grandson of a peer, and after two deaths might have become Viscount Dundreary. But all he had besides his Army pay at the time of his marriage was an approximate income of £500 a year, which, of course, in the hasty marriage settlements, he had bestowed on Isobel. So that, whether or not she grieved for Ronnie more than a month or two, she had gained £500 a year by her marriage. Miss Burgess had died at Pretoria of psychoenteritis whilst they were on their honeymoon, so there were no further obligations on her account, except a rather sensationally designed and lettered gravestone in the cemetery.

Lady Isobel Drumhaven, however, did not return to England when and because she became a widow. She thought more than once of tackling Rhodes at Groot-

LADY ISOBEL DRUMHAVEN

schuur, but he was obviously very ill, and efficiently guarded. However, her daring, her marriage, her family connections, the two losses she had sustained of husband and governess, her occasional printed articles, and her press quarrel with *The Times* had obtained her considerable sympathy and backing in the Transvaal. There, then, if you stayed six months, you became, as it were, a privileged person, a citizen, believer in the immense future of South Africa.

Isobel even, as a press correspondent, interviewed enemy generals. Some of the latest articles were almost pro-Boer in sentiment. She thought vaguely when the South African fuss was all over of riding across Rhodesia to the heart of Africa, of crossing the continent from the Cape to Cairo, as a young widow with a revolver and a stern smile.

But the tsetse-fly of the northern Limpopo and the Zambezi valley seemed to balk such projects, as she had no desire to trudge beside an ox-waggon.

So at last, when the treaty was signed, she came back to England, glorying in her widowhood and showing great impatience with Ronnie's female relations who wished to cry over her and him. Her own people were being rather hard hit over Irish properties and politics, over a fall in the price of English agricultural produce, and London rents. Her book on the South African campaign promised well, but somehow never got completed.

She played bridge between 1903 and 1905 with extraordinary asperity, and generally with gain. She took up suffrage after 1907 with malice and extravagant energy and clamour, but somehow just missed being arrested and going for trial. She generally went to the South of France instead, with health as an excuse.

In 1912-13 she had a scandal (really a violent quarrel) with a man much younger than herself, whom she had tried to compromise so as to oblige him to break off his engagement with a charming girl.

When the Great War broke out she at once attached herself—unasked—to some motor conveyance which ran about supplying—or pretending to supply—afternoon tea to the troops at the expense of a South African racing millionaire.

She became such a confounded nuisance to the Army and the Staff Corps and the Higher Command in Italy, whither she found her way, that a great general had the supreme courage to send her home and confront questions in the press and the Legislature.

She is now not more than forty-two. Extravagances in eating and drinking, indulgences in cocaine and morphia, and excessive cigarette-smoking have long since been given up, out of her dry-mouthed desire to live as long as possible. She has, I should think, an iron constitution. At eighty she may attract friends and be revered for her inaccurate and prejudiced memories of the Victorian, Edwardian, and Georgian reigns.

THE BROWSMITHS

IF you or I had a surname like Browsmith we should probably either change it or modify it by a notice in the papers, or do something glorious to redeem it and establish it; or, if of the female sex, marry to change it. But then you and I are rather exceptional people, acutely sensitive, swayed by the finest feelings. The original Mr. Browsmith of my narrative—H. Jesser Browsmith, as he wrote down his name, in early days—was not of quite such a fine order, though he was dimly stirred to action by a sense of something uninspiring in his surname.

Miss Cecilia Ponderson was so exceedingly anxious to be married that she cared little what patronymic she assumed, so long as she could precede it by "Mrs." She had been bequeathed by her grandmother's will well-invested funds, which at 4 to 5 per cent. produced an income of £2,500 a year. But this fortune was only to be hers on condition that she married before attaining the age of thirty-five. Should she remain a spinster after that age, the money passed to an orphanage.

Her grandmother died shortly after she had attained twenty-one years of age. Her mother, as soon as she had attended duly to the obsequies of her parent, set out on the quest of a son-in-law, and, to anticipate a point in my story, eventually secured her prey in the person of the above-mentioned H. Jesser Browsmith, who was a clerk in the Local Government Board on a salary of £450 a year.

"But," you will feel inclined to interpose, "with an income of £2,500 she might have aspired to something very much better, unless Mr. Browsmith was extraordinarily handsome, the heir to a peerage, or of great muscular strength. Did the girl drop her aitches?"

No. She spoke with great precision, and had learnt to do so at a very superior Ladies' School, facing Clapham Common. She had, in fact, received an expensive and extensive education. Her mother seemed a decent sort enough, I was told, by those who knew her. The £2,500 a year began with her grandmother, who lived on Clapham Common in a house standing in its own grounds of two acres. I never heard who her grandfather was; or, rather, I heard so many extraordinary names suggested, on the wrong side of the blanket, such ancient scandal about the younger sons of George the Third, that I felt further inquiry indecorous. The old lady at Clapham Common had died some years before I met her daughter and granddaughter; so also had the girl's father, who, I understood, had been on the Stock Exchange. It was somewhere about 1894 that Mrs. Ponderson—that was the name—Mrs. Ponderson and her daughter began to appear at dinner-parties in Marylebone, Regent's Park, and St. John's Wood. If you were entrapped into meeting them, there was some man present who told you that, on the day Miss Ponderson married, she would step into a clear £2,500 a year.

One look at her was generally sufficient for most men—sufficient to deter them from the adventure. It was not that she was sensationally ugly. Staggeringly ugly women, ogresses in-grain, lurid witches, fateful Nornas, get married with as much ease as houris and airy, faëry Lilians. Miss Ponderson was so common, so mean-looking. She had not a redeeming feature: muddy, shiny complexion; insufficient hair screwed back, screwed up, yet escaping in untidy wisps; green eyes with a slight tendency to red eyelids and watery conjunctiva; misplaced front teeth with indications of decay; a nose which turned red at the tip if excitement ensued; a shrill laugh (terribly aggravated by champagne); and a rather short, dumpy stature. She was badly though expensively dressed. . . .

For my part, if I refrained from averting my eyes I only looked again in pity whilst she renewed her inharmonious, shattering laughter.

Then years went by, and I was married and living in London. At some meeting of the Royal Geographical or the Zoological Society somebody said introductorily, "Mr. Jesser Browsmith—um—um—um." I turned on his indication and was introduced to Mr. Jesser Browsmith, a tall, angular, carefully dressed, *pince-nez*-ed, nearly middle-aged young man with a colourless face and a neutral tinted moustache. He, in his turn, mumbled something, bowed, and concluded by introducing "My wife."

At these words a dumpy little woman at his heels turned round and said, "I think we've met before, years ago, at the Paravesis'." I then found that Mr. Jesser Browsmith had married—had had the courage to marry—Miss Ponderson for her £2,500 a year (obviously). And had been trying for the last five years to do his duty by her. "Dear mamma," I gathered, in taking up the threads, had retired to a country cottage on the outskirts of a Suffolk town.

Miss Ponderson as Mrs. Browsmith had certainly improved in appearance since 1894. Her head and neck were surmounted by a dark brown hair confection from a good shop, probably in Sloane Street. Her weak eyes were disguised and helped by well-chosen *pince-nez*. Her front teeth were either pivoted or wholly false; they were at any rate unobjectionable. Her colourless complexion had wisely been left colourless. Her dress, though a little too "rich," was the work of an artist in clothing. The one outstanding feature of the former Miss Ponderson was the terrible laugh. I provoked it by some well-meant sally, and three or four startled men of science looked round.

However, after that I talked of the gravest things, and though I did not move her to tears I induced no excuse for merriment.

They called on us; we called on them—in Seymour Street. They had one peaky little daughter, and must have enjoyed an income of over £3,000 a year, for he—I saw in a book of reference—drew by now £600 a year from the Local Government Board.

By 1905 Mr. Jesser Browsmith had substituted for his *pince-nez* spectacles a single eyeglass with a black ribbon. The equipment, if not so useful, was far more distinguished looking. It really, the next year, secured him a slight advancement in his office.

The Browsmiths one evening, after an early dinner,

took us to the opera. Mrs. Jesser Browsmith had become a subscriber. She had a box there. Whether in her heart she cared for music and was not tone-deaf, I could never tell. But the opera seemed to her a distinguishment. She behaved according to code—was intensely silent during any utterance of voice or instrument, had books of the music as well as of the inane translation of the Italian words.

She had not had a bad education at Clapham, and so in time she got a nodding acquaintance with Italian, which she spoke with a Clapham accent. She had learnt after several seasons to discriminate the opera notabilities in an Italian way—"La Strozzi" (in reality Frau Strauss of Vienna), "Il Tortolo," "Le Brizzichetti," or the "fanciulla Bobinoglio" (thirty years old, but still operatically a child).

In 1909 her husband, by dint of hard work, the eyeglass, and the black ribbon, and some temporary usefulness in preparing a Bill, received unexpected promotion. He became "Sir Henry Browsmith"—an official friend advised him to drop the Jesser business—"very middle-class name."

His wife, whom he had not had time or indiscretion to prepare for the news, nearly swooned when he told her he was to be made a K.C.V.O. She was said to have arranged a private thanksgiving service at St. Paul's, Knightsbridge. Thereafter, they moved south from Seymour Street to Montpelier Square, and Lady Browsmith resolved to have her laugh "treated." Her husband, called on for advice after his knighthood, in a new mood of bland assertiveness had suggested this. So three times a week for several months, Lady Browsmith took lessons in rippling laughs, refined chuckling, and restrained outbursts of modish glee.

One way and another, Cecilia Browsmith was very like any other woman of the same class and age in 1911. She had corrected what was wrong and supplied much that was lacking. She went to the Coronation in Westminster Abbey, and when it was over reverted to the tight and skimpy skirts that had become the fashion.

But a further preoccupation possessed her mind and gradually dominated it. She began to believe herself of Royal descent. Her mother in Suffolk was dying—we all have to do that, sooner or later. In Mrs. Ponderson's case it was a little sooner (she was sixty-nine) than it might have been, had she paid more attention to diet. However, she was, when Cecilia came, irretrievably dying, and she told her daughter in a very faint voice that she had reason to believe herself the daughter of one of the younger sons of George the Third. Cecilia's grandmother, the old lady of Clapham Common, had been a young housekeeper to the prince, and it was through that liaison that the money endowment had come.

Then Mrs. Ponderson's speech became incoherent, and in three more days she was dead.

Thereafter Lady Browsmith swelled into dignity. Of course, she wore mourning for her mother, but it was State mourning. She told her husband everything, and much more than she had gathered from her mother, confirmatory evidence that her fertile mind had invented. After a fortnight's reticence till the funeral was over, and every seemly attention had been paid to the deceased lady, including the proving of her will by which the Browsmiths were fifteen hundred a year richer, Cecilia Browsmith began to develop her plans. There was her one little daughter—a morganatic princess, so to speak. Unhappily in ignorance of their Royal strain, she had been named "Gladys," quite a modern name, not included in the ten or eleven names bestowed on any remembered, civilised princess.

Steps must be taken before she came of age to give her the name of Frederica. Some such steps were taken without rousing any particular clamour in the other houses of Montpelier Square. Friends and guests were informed with some emphasis that the former Gladys had, in accordance with testamentary provisions of her grandmother's will, assumed the name of Frederica.

Most of the informed merely nodded. Frederica at the time was scarcely more than twelve—thirteen—a thin, pale, studious, obedient little girl, growing out of littleness into lankiness, obliged to wear glasses to aid her defective or contorted sight. One or two City men or officials said casually, " 'Frederica,' hey! What a deuce of a bore. What brought your grandmother to light? Thought she died years and years ago?"

"So she did, but—my dear mother—in her dying moments—remembered the wish and asked me—to give—effect—to it."

"Ah! Just so! Awful bore these female fancies about names. Well! Let's hope Gladys—wasn't that her name?—Gladys will be just as happy as Frederica. S'pose you'll call her 'Freddy'? Now I must finish up with your husband, because I've got to be back in the City by three-thirty."

When Frederica was fourteen in the spring of the war year, she seemed to be out-growing her strength. The specialist to whom she was submitted looked at her with rather a serious face when he had concluded his *questionnaire*. "Life in the country, my dear Lady Browsmith—in the country—in the *country* is what our little friend wants—country air, downs rather than hilltops—pretty scenery—but not too chilly or wet. . . . Some part of Surrey, eh? Or Sussex or North Hants? Never mind about the education, so long as she has learnt to read and write. I'll prescribe a tonic and several other things. But country air is the main cure. . . ."

This was rather a blow to Lady Browsmith's schemes. Yet it had its countervailing advantages. She was spending, one way and another, £200 a year on Frederica's education. The same sum should surely pay the rent of a decent country house in the regions suggested. It was time they began to prepare the home and retiring place of their old age when Henry's pension would go far to replace his loss of salary. And no doubt Rica would grow strong by the time she was sixteen or seventeen, and could then resume her studies. Girls, too, seldom nowadays married till they were well past twenty-one. . . .

So—fortunately just before the War—there began for Rica the one, short, happy time she was to know. A kindly governess, who was also a nice-looking, well-bred woman, was engaged to look after her, Lady Browsmith having to be so much in town just then.

Next came the War. Frederica was very sorry about the War, but she did not think of it so closely at first, in her passionate desire to get well and strong, and be able to study closely the subjects that interested her. As she lay out on a warm rug on the down behind the house in the September sunshine, or sat on a low chair gazing steadfastly into a scented wood fire in a rainy October or chilly November—as Miss Marett read aloud the day's paper, or old stories of eighteenth-century France, *The Arabian Nights,* German fairy-tales, *Hans Andersen,* or some good, modern novel or equally good Thackerayan romance of the eighteen-fifties—she took in half of what was being read; but her thoughts were partly out at the seat of war, thinking of what the children were suffering in the villages and the soldiers in the trenches.

Her health grew better for the time. Ashamed of inaction, she taught herself to knit; Miss Marett taught her to prepare lint, at her earnest request. Together they got quite busy through the winter, preparing all manner of war-hospital necessities, comforts, and amusements for convalescence.

In the early spring—1915—Miss Marett heard there were wounded soldiers at Guildford, convalescents who were allowed on fine days to come to friendly houses and be entertained. She invited a party of six to start with, as Rica was a little shy—shy at suspecting herself of being ugly and awkward.

In this respect she was right: she was a poor ugly duckling, and timidity, lack of assurance, made her hand shake so that she could not hand a teacup without risk of a clatter or a spill. But to all discerning minds, to the mind of a soldier of thirty, of a woman of education who had known great sorrows (like Miss Marett), to a farmer who had tried to make a profit out of British agriculture, Frederica was seen to have a mind and a disposition fraught with loving-kindness behind the grotesque face with its look of pain, the bowed shoulders suggesting spinal trouble. She had something here in her face and her disposition that her mother lacked; perhaps less so, her grandmother. Her father had no vice, but he had no heart. He was a slave to form, to the office desk and all that appertained thereto.

Lady Browsmith might have felt the disappointment about her daughter's health far more than she did, owing to the outburst of the Great War. The King's action in proclaiming his House as the House of Windsor shattered her pride in the rill of Brunswick blood which—she imagined—coursed in her veins. It had become not merely indelicate but disloyal to trace back one's descent from the Hanoverian dynasty. Queen Victoria, whatever may have been her origin, had founded a new dynasty, had earned by a reign of sixty-four years a claim to special consideration. Victoria and her grandchildren were only collateral relations of hers; they had founded the House of Windsor in which she played no part. . . .

"I think, my dear," said her husband to her one day in 1916, "we will—ah—*drop* the subject, don't you know? I notice people are a little inclined to laugh about your prepossession, and that would never do, now that I am head of my department."

So the matter of the possibly quite mythical Hanoverian descent of Cecilia Browsmith gradually died away.

She alluded to it twice in 1918, once—with a little shudder—in 1919, never—to my knowledge—since.

We saw increasingly little of her since the beginning of the War. Chance rather than intention brought us into closer touch with Helen Marett and Rica Browsmith. The parents of the latter were so much occupied with war-work that they very seldom came and stayed at Knaresfield, the house on the down near Godalming. But we were drawn into that neighbourhood in 1917 over matters it would be tedious here to describe, and came to know both Helen and poor sickly, ugly Frederica. Their home, indeed, became a place of pleasant resort. I had come to know of a very sad episode in Helen's life in 1913, against the remembrance of which she fought bravely. (She is happy, now, I am glad to think.) And I felt really interested in Rica and her incurable spine trouble. As she ripened, became adolescent and mature, she developed a most charming nature; she lost her shyness with sympathetic people whom she liked. She could see the humour which hung about her mother's disappointment, and the gradual turning of her father into a piece of office furniture, and the glorified episode of a great-grandmother's frailty. When Helen told us of her death last September—her mother and father were in Switzerland—we felt a real pang of regret. I should like to believe in Immortality, if only to feel I was still in touch with the spirit of Rica Browsmith.

ADELA TOTWORTHY

WHAT tragedy lies in English surnames! Those of Anglo-Saxon America are as odd, extraordinary, aristocratic, and laughable, but public opinion takes them for granted and refuses to mock or wonder. No one would think of saying to you in the United States, "Excuse me, but you have a *very* extraordinary name." It would be ruled out as an inquisitive and impolite remark, even in the roughest quarter of New York or Los Angeles.

But at home names matter to a terrible degree. Many young women make foolish marriages to change their surnames; many a worthy young man, who might have made Miss Fitzhardinge or Mary Foljambe happy, is refused because acceptance would have meant changing her surname to Brassband, Bellingcoop, or Mullingtoe.

Adela Totworthy's life seemed likely to be a case in point. Her mother, a dear, placid elderly lady, was the widow of an east-country clergyman. *She* never gave her husband's surname a thought. Her own had been Brown. She had come down to stay with the Squire's family in the early 'seventies (having been at school with one of the daughters), and had seemed to the young Vicar a very suitable person to propose to. So he had proposed; and she with little demur had accepted him. She brought him about £150 a year as her dowry. They had only one child surviving—Adela—and when the Vicar died in the early 'nineties, his widow gathered up all he left which was realisable and with it purchased an annuity of £400 a year. So on £550 income—in those days quite a comfortable sum—they settled in a charming little house with a lovely garden at Little Swadlingcombe, three miles from the coast in the north of Suffolk.

I met Adela in the autumn of 1901, when I came down to spend a week-end with the old Squire. One of his sons had been with me in Central Africa, had rushed off to join in the fight with the Boers, and had been killed in the Transvaal. We had tennis on the Saturday afternoon, and Adela Totworthy had bicycled over—five miles —to play. When they told me she was coming, of course, I said mechanically, "What an extraordinary name!" and Mary Melchet, the Squire's youngest daughter, interposed: "Oh, *don't* say that! At least, I mean, don't make any *comment* she can hear. She is so *absurdly* sensitive on the subject."

Of course, I acquiesced; but on account of the name, I scanned her appearance with the more interest. She must have been scarcely older than twenty-one, and was so distinctly good-looking that I wondered to meet her unmarried, and in Suffolk, where the marriage rate is high.

I was led to talk her over with the Squire on the following Sunday afternoon. "Adela," he said—"she gets savage if I call her 'Addie,'' though she was born within half a mile of our doors—well, then, Adela is a *goose*. Her mouth is getting a peevish droop, all because of her surname and her inability to change it. What does a surname matter? Especially in a woman who is more or less able to marry. But she's very personable, and for aught I know a good girl and not a fool, except in regard to her name. . . . Yet she can't get any one to propose—at least any one she deems worthy of acceptance. As far as I can make out—though, goodness knows, I've quite enough of my own troubles to attend to— she's refused since she was nineteen two or three young farmers —who'd have taken her over with only £50 a year pin-money—as 'not good enough,' 'not what she could call *gentlemen.*' . . . What *rot!* Makes one sick. But don't let's waste our time discussing her. . . ."

I came away on the Monday afternoon, and Adela Totworthy passed into the second or third rank of people interesting to contemplate. Three years went by. Squire Melchet of Middlehampton Park was killed in a bad hunting accident. His eldest son succeeded him, and his three daughters came to live in London to take up professions.

One day I was dining with Samuelson at the newly opened Ritz Hotel, where an unusually choice type of dinner was then given. At a table near by, so far as I could distinguish faces in the green gloom, sat Adela Totworthy. Her hostess was a rather handsome woman with a tired face and much jewellery, and her host was a somewhat Oriental type of man, whom in some aspects you might have called good looking. He had Eastern eyes with long eyelashes, a slightly—very slightly—hooked nose, splendid teeth, glossy hair, and silky moustache. His cheeks and chin gave the suggestion that the beard required shaving twice a day if it was not to make the lower part of his face too blue.

Samuelson was telling me how he captured the Tory seat at Spitalhampton. It was, no doubt, an exciting story to listen to in 1904, but I gave it no more than polite attention. The two people with Adela interested me more. I distinctly liked the woman and as distinctly *dis*liked the man. Who were they, and what should I do about Adela? Greet her? Our eyes met, and I effected a modest bow. She was evidently pleased, and waved a hand almost effusively, explaining her discovery to her hosts.

I never even then cared much for wine; so Samuelson, when the other diners had reached dessert, proposed adjournment to the smoking-room of the Reform Club, where he would tell me of the fight in greater detail and the coming down of the Liberal leaders. We rose to go, or, at least, I did, while Samuelson was paying his bill. I instinctively crossed the two or three yards to Adela's table. She seemed evidently pleased at my coming, or I should merely have bowed and passed on. It was thus I came to hear her host's name. Mr. "Rasselas," it sounded like. Mr. Rasselas, I was told, had passed much of his youth in the East, and had presumably made a large fortune. "*Now* he is trying to settle down in Suffolk, near the Melchets' place—Dovercourt, you know; and I am sure our climate will suit—Margaret—Mrs. Rasselas. . . . Baghdad has *quite* exhausted her!" said Adela.

She herself was looking her best. There was a natural

colour in her cheeks (I thought), her eyes sparkled, and she was very effectively dressed. They were going on shortly to a screamingly funny piece that began at nine. Adela was staying with them at the Ritz.

More years passed. I met no-longer-young Colonel Melchet one afternoon, just before the Coronation. He was attending it in some capacity. "What has become of Miss—Miss—— Bless my soul, I *ought* to remember her name! Not 'Topheavy,' Tot—Tot—*I* know! *Tot-worthy?*" I asked.

"Adela?"

"Yes; that was her Christian name."

"Well, it seems to us rather sad. She's been infatuated for years by a bounder of a fellow who bought Dovercourt—ten or eleven miles from here—seven years ago. Odd sort of name—Abyssinian, Baghdadi, Armenian—*I* don't know what. But his father settled in England long ago. His people made any amount of money out of the Turkish Government. Some say he's a Kurd in origin, but I expect he is some kind of a Jew. However, he supports the Church of England, and has subscribed to the fund we're getting up for a Bishop of Suffolk. His wife and Adela became tremendous pals years ago. Now the poor woman is dying of cancer—so they say— and Addie almost lives there. . . . Her mother's dead, by the way, and she only has about two hundred a year to live on, so I hope the Rasselases give her something. . . . Come down and shoot some partridges in the autumn, when all this fuss is over."

I accepted, and went in September, less for the partridges than for some interest in Suffolk scenery and a quavering fancy to inquire into the affairs of Adela. I had always regretted that a woman so good-looking, and well-dressed on small means, had not made a happy marriage. . . .

A groom drove me over one afternoon. Colonel Melchet still hesitated to embark on a motor, and clung to his horses. Mrs. Rasselas, I was informed, was not very well, but Miss Totworthy was in, and would see me. . . . Mr. Rasselas was out shooting with a party. . . .

The house was magnificent, though rather overdone in splendour of furniture. Adela came running into the library where I was deposited. If she was twenty-one in 1901, she must now be thirty-one. But she did not look it—did not seem older than twenty-five. . . .

Her manner was not staid—slightly feverish in gaiety —eyes always seemed ready to stray from your face and look for some one else. . . . However, I stayed for tea, and with the tea came in Mrs. Rasselas. She looked to me still handsome—enigmatic—complexion pale because evidently she had ceased to "make up." Adela (I saw, in the clear light of a September afternoon) was made up —very skilfully.

The shooting party came in when I had finished my tea. Rasselas was quite civil, seemed even anxious to make a good impression on me, pressed me to come on from Middlehampton and join his party. But this I could not do, though I consented to come and see him in London, later on.

In the following June Mrs. Rasselas died. Adela, I

gathered, was distracted with grief. She had for some months been living at Dovercourt, and had let her little house at Swadlingcove. Of course, she had to go back there soon after the funeral. In the September of that year (1912) I found Rasselas at the London meetings, which were to try to effect a reconcilement of Anglo-German ambitions, but which, as we know, proved futile. I thought he took an unusually prominent part, and seemed for once eager to bring an understading.

In the spring of 1913 we were staying at Queen Anne's Mansions, and Mary Melchet came in to see us one morning. "You remember Adela Totworthy?" she said. "I've had *such* a time with her! Really, I don't care to follow up all my deductions. . . . It isn't proper for an unmarried woman to do so! But this is where she is staying for a day or two. You professed a half-humorous interest in her once. Your wife is a most kindhearted person. . . . Perhaps *you* could intervene?"

We went to the hotel, near Portland Place. We found a very dishevelled, hysterical Adela, much of her good looks washed off by tears, and the lids of her fine eyes reddened. . . . We gathered then—and afterwards— that she had come up to London, as she had often done before, to dine with Rasselas and—I am afraid—to sleep at his London house. Either she had called on him desperately to marry her, and he had got sick of her assiduity, or—or—well, there were twenty explanations, all of which we two discussed with futile curiosity. At any rate about midnight he had had a taxi summoned—or she had —and in this she had driven in choking wrath to the

Portland Place hotel (a most respectable one), arriving in an extravagant dinner dress, with nothing whatever in the way of luggage. They had politely but firmly declined to give her a room. She had, with equal firmness, but without much politeness, refused to be ejected, and sat—beautifully dressed, but a little dishevelled—in the great hall, until at five in the morning the night manager had in pity assigned her a room.

At eight o'clock the next morning she had got the management to lend her six-pence, and had dispatched a telegram to Mary Melchet.

The only explanation she attempted when my wife returned with a lent day-dress for her to wear on the journey home was: "I might have been a very different woman if I had been born a Templecombe—or even a Tadcaster."

What was the solution? The Canary Islands, a trip to Tenerife. My idea. She had a clear £200 a year from her inherited trust securities—a fortune in those days—also a nice little house to sell, a fine outfit of clothes, and numerous valuable odds and ends. She went out to Tenerife and found the very place to suit her at Orotava. She has turned it into a private hotel, which is bringing her in quite a large income. But she has never married, and has refused many offers. She has learnt Spanish, is much respected and always known as "Dona Adela." The Spaniards decided "Totworthy" was unpronounceable and no improvement.

Rasselas—of course, I do not give his real name—

went out to Baghdad in 1914, and when the Great War broke out, resumed Turkish nationality and took the German side. He has by now lost nearly all his fortune, and lives on a small income at Konia.

THE TASK

HIS task of eighteen years lay finished and under his eyes, a great pile of paper—typescript and manuscript—completed down to the word "finis," which he had added that morning with a half-humorous deviation into the rut of the conventional. There it was, with the last necessary red-ink annotation or underlining to express peculiar type, with all its diagrams, the rough and the finished designs for its maps and illustrations. For a man of his temperament—so eager to arrive at results that he was sometimes slipshod in his progress—the work was singularly neat. Again and again a badly written word was pasted over with stamp paper, and a clear version of the letters written thereon, so that the reasonably educated printer and printer's reader might be met half-way, and press corrections avoided as far as possible.

In time long gone by, encouraged by the vogue of his more superficial work, he had been accustomed to conclude bargains with publishers or editors before pen had been put to paper, and to send off his stuff to the printers as it issued sheet after sheet from his brain, scribbled in pencil, splashed and blotted with quill pens, or almost illegible in the scrabble of steel nibs, or shockingly typed by the clumsy fingers of the amateur in typewriting. But *the* Task of his life, the one great work of which he could never feel ashamed—work surely that must take and hold for a time the first place in the treatment of its subject—had been completed down to the last detail before going to a firm of publishers which itself from ancientry and achievements had become a kind of religious guild. Again and again during the eighteen years the earlier work had been rewritten and revised, so that the opening chapters were, if possible, more recent in spirit and outlook than the terminal, which contained his general conclusions—conclusions arrived at in the very inception of the work—brilliant guesses subsequently confirmed by long and patient examination of facts.

This June morning the work lay finished. In the afternoon, if he possessed the necessary energy, it would be most carefully packed, and perhaps he, himself, or at any rate a trusted member of his household, would convey it by rail and cab to the very arcanum of the great publishing firm which was to produce it. The question of the terms of publication had been barely discussed: it was so certain that the work would come up to the standard of the publishers, that it would be an ultimate success from a commercial point of view, and that the dealings between publisher and author would be on lines of perfect probity. Moreover, though not precisely a rich man and spending lavishly all he could afford to spend on scientific research, he cared comparatively little for wealth but egregiously for fame and reputation. To him it was the only certain form of immortality, and a measured immortality at best—the preservation of his name and individuality from oblivion three or four centuries ahead—perhaps more, if the world's progress were interrupted by no cataclysm, great or little.

THE TASK

And now in the reaction of accomplishment he began to ask himself whether it was worth while, whether he had chosen the better part. Eighteen years before, he had been left a small fortune and had virtually retired from professional life and from the holding of a Government appointment in order to devote himself with ever-increasing absorption of mind and body to the Task, the task of setting forth a great thesis, a work in biology which should make him, if he were fairly treated, another Darwin in the world's estimation, and not a supplanter but a supplementer of that originator of the New Bible. With three to four thousand pounds a year from his own prudent investments he had withdrawn himself from the world of London, Oxford, Manchester, and Edinburgh, to live in the most perfect country solitude he could find within two hours' railway journey of London. He was a well-known figure at Kew, in Regent's Park, in the Botanical Gardens of Cambridge and even Edinburgh, and a member of nearly all the serious scientific societies of Great Britain, but a member who seldom attended meetings and only sent his contributions to be printed in their journals. Though at one time popular in many circles with both men and women, even noteworthy as an athlete in his young-man days, he had long ceased to appear at parties given by the State or by great personages in the social world.

He was president, vice-president, or patron of a variety of local societies and clubs, but his connection with them had gradually dwindled to the annual allocation of as many guineas as he could somewhat grudgingly afford. His estate was of modest dimensions, but on the whole well ordered, both in house and grounds, except for the unavoidable untidiness, litter, and ramshackle effects of his biological experiments, his photography, and his failures.

But was it worth while? Turning his thoughts back over the last few years of his life, he found himself now at the point where middle age passes into old age, almost without a friend, with scarcely any one left to him for whom he felt warm human love, or by whom he was certain to be loved for himself alone and not for his power of bestowing benefits. He recalled the friendships of his youth and the prime of manhood, even of his early middle age. Where were those friends now? Most of them were dead, and in the last years of their life their friendship had faded before his own retirement and absorption. They were not interested in his Task, could not help him with it, did not come within its scope, or were jealous of his close application and coming renown. Or they had died before friendship had dwindled, and he was haunted by some very dear memories—memories of sisters, brothers, aunts, college friends, brother officials, former sweethearts and Egerias, of whom it seemed to him he might have seen much more in the later years of their life, but who were now gone from him for ever. Only that night he had been searching through old packets of documents and letters carefully ribboned and stored (with a pretty imitation of official meticulousness) by the hand of his dead wife. He was hunting for one or two half-forgotten notes relating to his Task, and the sight of these dead handwritings had harrowed him with the mental pictures they called up. Here were the letters of an aunt, who had been to him as a second mother. Yet he had not even gone to her funeral because he could not tear himself away from watching an experiment which it had taken him two years to prepare.

Other letters reminded him with a wry smile of the quarrels of two of his dearest friends, as near neighbours as he allowed himself in his carefully chosen retreat; friends themselves for years, but both touched with a crankiness born in India. They had become deadly enemies over a boundary ditch. People had said at the time that a few words from him on either side would have disposed of this bone of contention; and the happy reunion of all three households as in the past might have indefinitely continued. But he had said to himself at the time, in his early widowerhood, that he would take no concern, undergo no further agitation regarding other people's affairs: they must quarrel and make it up, or not, as they chose, even if they drifted away out of the neighbourhood and out of his life. He must finish his Task, and to grapple with its problems apply to it every ounce of mental energy that he possessed.

This he said to himself, in recovering from the greatest blow which Fate had dealt him—the loss of his wife. The marriage had been an early one on both sides, of convinced affection, of ardent love indeed, which had paled as the years went by in its fervour on his side, as he had drawn himself more and more into the cloistral life. Within a fortnight after his wife's death he had applied himself with ever-increasing rigour to his studies and his Task, obstinately resolved at any rate not to lose the shadow in addition to the substance.

Yet even now he asked himself whether, viewed through the mentality of a God—if there were a God—he had acted wrongly in his ant-like policy. His wife, it is true, had died of what was then called an incurable disease, but it was originated by heartbreak. Their only son had behaved disgracefully in his early manhood. He, the father, had paid his debts, and to give him a new start in life, and at any rate efface all scandal which might have cast a shadow over the Task, had supplied several thousand pounds out of his capital to give him an honourable career in a distant colony.

The boy, not inherently bad, had done well in the land to which he had been exiled. Two or three times a year he exchanged a rather formal correspondence with his father—had indeed offered to pay back by degrees the funds which had opened to him lucrative pursuits in a new land. The father had replied to this—all affection for his son having long ago been killed not only by disappointment at his behaviour, but quite equally by absorption in the Task—by a formal note of quittance cancelling the debt. The son, on his part, obviously cared little for his father, and was utterly out of sympathy with his pursuits.

All this might have been very different if he had devoted himself to the training and education of this son without intermission from his schooldays to the completion of his college career and his adoption of a profession.

But the Task had absorbed him, and the son had sought friendship and sympathy in other directions.

So, also, with his daughters. Both of them had married; the younger he had loved with a rare intensity. She

THE TASK

had made a happy marriage, but a year afterwards had died in her confinement; and he, with no presage of disaster, had not even been with her at the time—had, in fact, seen little or nothing of her during the last three months of her life, absorbed in his researches and thinking it would be quite time enough to put himself out to visit her or have her to visit him, when all the fuss of the confinement was over and she was once more the normal woman.

The other daughter took after her brother's disposition. She was well married and to a kindly, indulgent husband of good standing in the near neighbourhood, so that she was virtually able to look after her father's house as well as her own. She would probably soon be with him at the little cottage on the outskirts of his grounds wherein most of his work was done. But she would come with her hard, bright eyes and brisk manner, contemptuous of the importance of the Task, and only regretting the "father who, after all, had a decent income and came of known people" —on the fringe, even, of great families—did not play a greater part in the county, and was not more useful to herself, her husband, and her children as a social factor.

There he was at sixty—deeply respected, it might be, by several old and faithful servants, who had aided him in his researches till they stood outside the ranks of mere domestics, but loved by no one, and his own loves in the grave.

Was it worth while? Had he paid too great a price for such poor immortality as we are sure of?

And with some inconsistency and a half-unconscious sob and catch of the breath, he said to himself, "No!"